Laura Koerber

LIMBO

Published by Who Chains You Publishing
P.O. Box 581
Amissville, VA 20106

www.WhoChainsYou.com

Ghost art by the author, Laura Koerber
Book cover and interior design by Tamira Thayne

ISBN-13: 978-1-946044-17-4

Printed in the United States of America

First Edition

To my sister, Anne, with gratitude

TABLE OF
Contents

CHAPTER ONE:

Alyse and Trey

Alyse watched Trey drift across the dry grass, his long legs dangling like laundry from a clothesline. She had seen him float by before, up the dirt road toward the line of willows that edged the river, back down the dirt road to the village, up again. Trey was gregarious, but not talkative. He probably wanted someone to invite him to hang around for awhile, just hang in mutual silence.

He was nearly past her shack when she called out to him, "Hey, Trey."

He pivoted slowly, his head ducked down. Trey was shy.

"Where're you headed?" She knew as soon as the words left her mouth that she'd asked the wrong question. Trey had no destination.

He shrugged, looking down at the dirt and grass. "Just taking a walk."

She said, "I'm just sitting here." That's all she could

offer.

Trey floated up to her front steps, letting his legs drift through the grass. He hung in the air, uncertainly, until she asked, "Do you want to sit down?"

Seemed like she ought to give him something—a Coke, water, or beer—since he was an adult, but the social niceties of life no longer applied.

Trey draped himself on the steps, his bare feet in the dirt. He gave her a small smile. "So how're ya doin'?" His voice was gritty, full of the dust and scrub of Texas.

She shrugged, then decided to tell the truth, or something close to it. "I'm OK most of the time because what else can you do? But sometimes I'm really, really pissed off. It sucks, OK? Not fair."

"Yeah," he said with genuine sympathy. "You're just a young thing, and you ain't been here that long."

"Yeah." She looked down at her long legs, once brown and muscular, an athlete's legs, now vague and gray. Trey's legs sagged alongside hers, his feet flopped to the side. With a twinge of shame, Alyse remembered that she was talking to a man who had been a quadriplegic. She said, "I mean, I know I didn't get screwed any more than a lot of other people, but still I got screwed."

"Yeah," said Trey again, with resignation. He had been depressed in life and being dead had not improved his mood. Fortitude was both a virtue and a vice in Trey. Maybe that was why no one really wanted to hang with him; he was like a sad old dog. Alyse wanted to kick something or somebody. She wanted to rage at God. If there was one.

She gazed over the line of shacks, out across the yellow foothills toward the distant mountains, a dull grayish blue under the faded sun. The leaves of willows were silvery green and flashed in the light wind, the only brightness in the landscape.

She realized that she liked the silvery flashes. Then she thought, is that a blessing? One of those purported tender mercies The Preacher yapped about? Or just something pretty that God hadn't gotten around to messing up yet? If she let herself think about religion, she got very bitter, and the bitterness hurt. The weird thing was, she had not been brought up to be religious at all, so God, if there was one, had not failed to meet her expectations.

Trey, raised in a Bible-believing church, was stranded in Limbo, but had no anger.

Alyse leaned forward, her shoulders tightening. Trey shifted uneasily, embarrassed at his inability to comfort her. She thought, screw him, he doesn't know anything any more than anyone else.

She didn't have a lot of friends in the village. Some of the villagers were locked into depression or chronic grumpiness, or had the frenzied look of religious fanaticism. They were all older than her. She was seriously thinking of moving elsewhere, but Jack the Traveler said the road only led away, and no one could ever come back. He also said the places he'd been to weren't much different from where they were. It was all basically the same: wooden shacks in some places, tents or rundown tract houses in other places, but always villages of ghosts hanging around, exiled from the living. In between villages, the countryside was about the same everywhere, too: low, gently rounded hills, meandering rivers, groves of trees, impossibly distant mountains, a vast blue sky. Jack had tried to get to the mountains once, but they just kept moving farther and farther away.

Their village was a raggle-taggle series of dried-out, shriveled-up wooden shacks, paint long gone. Maybe the buildings had been like that from the day of creation. Or maybe once there had been paint, nails, and the possibility of repairs. If the people of the village were supposed to improve the properties, then God was seriously remiss for failing to provide them the wherewithal. On the other hand, no one had any reason to improve anything. They really didn't need buildings, after all. They could all be haunting the sagebrush, and it wouldn't make any difference in terms of physical well-being.

She had the cabin on the far western edge of the village. It was hers because no one else wanted it: just steps leading to an open door, one main room, and a collapsed back bedroom. She wished she could do something to brighten it up. The splintery brown walls were like a rebuke, as if she had done something to deserve being exiled from all she loved and from all she had expected from life.

Abruptly, Alyse stood up, an action that still felt strange: no pushing with hands or feet, no feeling of gravity. She just wafted upwards. Trey joined her.

"Let's go," she said.

"Go where?" Trey asked.

"How about to the river."

CHAPTER TWO:
Shall We Gather by the River

The river wasn't far. The geography of the area was simple: distant mountains to the east and west, prairie in between, a river to the south, the village a little ways up the road from the river.

Alyse flew in sudden starts and stops that reflected her mood. They swept over the sagebrush and through the willow thickets with no more disturbance than the breeze, Alyse first, with Trey trailing behind.

The river was narrow, nestled down between the willow-crowded banks, a dark, sinuous flow. Trey hung uncertainly in the air over the water. His lack of energy was like a black hole, dragging her down. She accelerated away from him, upriver, sliding though the air like a fish in water. Trey disappeared behind a bank of cottonwoods. Alyse did a pirouette in the air and reversed course. She waited impatiently for Trey to catch up.

"You must have been a track star back home," he teased, smiling sadly. Not angry at being left behind.

"I was," Alyse told him. She would've been angry if someone just flew off and left her. She didn't want to leave Trey again, but she did want to rebel against his hangdog demeanor.

"Let's go wading," she said, on impulse. "Didn't you do that when you were a kid?"

Alyse dropped down into the water on her hands and knees. She was startled by the sight of water flowing through her legs. She did not feel the cold. She could see the rocks beneath the water, at first just dark colors, but the more she looked, the more she saw: russet, maroon, purple, flashes of gold. She crawled around in the water, feeling it slide through her legs like blood through veins. She almost felt alive.

"How many colors do you see, Trey?" she asked.

"Uh." He joined her in the water, lowering himself awkwardly. "Lots of colors." His voice lifted a bit.

"Yeah." The sand between the rocks was glittery, tiny gems ever-changing in the refracted light. She noticed a fish.

"Hey, Trey, do you see that?"

"Yeah, I wish I had my fishing rod."

She had been thinking the same thing, but there was no point to fishing when you don't eat. Which she supposed was a good thing from the fish's perspective.

Was the fish watching them?

"Hey, Trey, I bet we can go clear under water."

"Yeah, maybe we could." He had been in the village much longer than her, but had never thought of going under the river water.

Alyse hunkered down into the water. The river flowed through her, gurgling and swishing, thick wet sounds of conversation, as if the river was talking to the willows and the rocks.

She would have submerged herself completely, but Trey, kneeling uneasily in the water, seemed to want to leave. She decided to come back to the river some other day without Trey. After all, she had an infinity of time on her hands. There was always going to be a tomorrow to get through.

They drifted up into the air over the water. Alyse noted that neither of them seemed to be wet.

"It's real pretty here," Trey said with wonder. Alyse looked around in surprise, absorbing the greenery and the cheerful gurgle of the water. The river and the willows were pretty when viewed from the air. Something else God has not taken from us yet, Alyse thought.

They rose further up into the sky. The trees and river merged together and wove themselves into the landscape, like a line of embroidery on a patchwork quilt. Alyse and Trey hung in the air, taking in the view. Then a touch of breeze wafted them away from the river toward the village.

From the sky, the prairie looked infinite. It was not a featureless prairie, but the features were subtle: an occasional grove of trees, a small rise or outcrop of rocks. Under the afternoon sun, a black spot of shadow lurked beneath every shrub and tree. Deer were in the shadows, invisible. Cows snoozed in a grove of cottonwoods. Pigs lolled in the underbrush.

The ramshackle dwellings of the village were huddled together, as if in solidarity against the vast prairie. A few ghosts were visible. Darla, the village busybody, was hanging in front of her house, hoping that something would happen. The Preacher was sitting on the steps of the old church. Emmanuel, who had the best voice in the village choir, was lolling out in the brush behind his shack—just standing, motionless.

The cats in the village were sleeping. Chickens foraged, pecking the ground like wonky sewing machines, clucking companionably to each other. Unlike the people, the chickens were always busy.

Alyse felt a pang of envy for the chickens. They seemed to know what they were doing. The rest of the day stretched in front of her: vast, blank, empty, devoid of meaningful choices. She had no idea what she was going to do with the long hours before nightfall.

Trey said, "You want to go over to Lily's with me? Sometimes we play cards."

Lily, Alyse thought, that mean Filipino lady. But she didn't have anything else to do.

"OK."

CHAPTER THREE:
Eights and Aces

Lily could sort of understand why she hadn't gone to Heaven, and she knew she didn't deserve Hell. She was marginally adjusted to an existence in a village that looked like an abandoned set for Hollywood Westerns. She had staked out a claim on the saloon.

Of course, she had to share it. Warren occupied one upstairs room and The Naked Man haunted the other, but she had established herself as mistress of the downstairs bar and gambling area. It was a good fit because one of her pleasures in life had been poker.

God had not provided playing cards, but Lily was resourceful; she had made her own cards by tearing off strips of wallpaper, and trimming them to more or less the same dimensions. She scratched crude numbers on the blank sides with mud on the end of a twig. The numbers had to be renewed regularly.

No face cards, just "J", "Q", and "K".

She dealt seven card stud. Anyone familiar with her deck could tell what the cards were by the particulars of the ragged edges. They used small rocks and sticks for chips, so everyone was rich. Cheating was appreciated, since it livened up what otherwise was a boringly risk-free game. Lily stood up to deal, elbows out, making a show, as she skimmed the cards to the players.

"Two up, one down, read 'em and weep."

She dealt herself a pair, hidden, and a queen, showing.

Jack said, "If you are going to cheat, can't you at least be subtle about it?" Jack had been handsome once, but he'd gone to seed before dying of heart disease.

"Hey, them's fighting words," Lily drawled, grinning with satisfaction.

Everyone knew she had not cheated. Not yet. They played on the floor as there was no furniture. Lily arranged herself neatly, legs tucked to one side, as she had been taught to sit in the Filipino farming village of her birth. Jack just sank waist deep into the floor, while Trey sprawled all over the place, as if he didn't know where his legs were. Warren, a former college professor, liked to hover in the lotus position. Alyse still had not figured out how she wanted to handle sitting or laying; it seemed pointless to act as if she had substance, yet she didn't like having parts of her body sag through the floor. She found, as most of them had, that, with effort, she could materialize parts of herself into somewhat solid form, so she attempted to sit cross-legged on the floor, as she would have done in life.

They were all concentrating on their fingers, on making their hands substantial enough to hold their cards.

"Ante up," Lily called out.

"I'll stay in." Trey tossed a pebble. The others followed.

"And here they come. We will see who Lady Luck loves." With a flourish, Lily laid down another card for each player. They were evaluating their hands when their game was interrupted by shouting from outside.

"What the Hell?" Jack's head jerked up in surprise. Shouting was rare in the village. Crying was common enough, though many did that alone, but most people didn't yell about anything. What was there to argue about?

They converged on the window.

Outside a scrappy little ghost was howling at The Chinese Lady. The Chinese Lady was stocky, middle-aged, and had a weirdly persistent smile, but no English. She kept to herself, mostly, in a shack on the far edge of town, where she lived with ten or eleven cats. The scrappy man was a stranger. He seemed to be drunk, staggering around, waving his arms. He was demanding answers from The Chinese Lady.

"What the Hell is this? Where is my truck? What the Hell did you do with my truck?"

Her response was loud but incomprehensible. Probably she was telling him to leave her alone.

"Get the Hell away from me, you chink! Get out of my way," the little guy hollered.

"That's Scotty," said Lily in a tone of disbelief. She swelled up visibly, like an angry toad. "That sonuvabitch."

"You know him?" Warren's eyebrows lifted in surprise. Warren was tall and elegant. Draped in an oversized hospital gown, he looked like a Roman Senator.

"He's my husband."

Lily balled herself up into a missile and shot through the wall out into the street. Scotty saw her flying at him and staggered backward.

"You bastard!" Lily yelled. "What are you doing here? Go away! No one wants you here!"

Scotty was speechless. He stepped back, windmilling his arms, his mouth opening and closing. Lily flew up into his face and hissed at him.

"You are going to stay away from me. You are going to stay out of my sight! Do you hear me?"

"Lily, oh my God, I'm having the DT's." Scotty rubbed his eyes. His hands disappeared into his face. "Oh, my God, help me."

"God isn't going to help you," Lily sneered. "You're dead, you jerk."

"Dead?" Scotty asked. "I ain't dead."

"Yes, you are. And you do not belong here! You belong in Hell!"

"Can I help?" It was The Preacher. He wasn't a real preacher. In life he had done some lay preaching in jails, the only place where people could be compelled to listen to him. About half of the village's population of thirty-two (now thirty-three) attended his weekly services, mostly out of boredom or for the singing.

He was an immature thirty, a potbellied man with curly blond hair: short, weak-faced, uneducated and ineffectual. Now he tried to intervene in the fight, tried to insert a firm reasonableness into his naturally high-pitched voice.

"Let's not fight, people. I'm sure this can be worked out."

"What the Hell do you know about it!" Lily screamed. She took a swing at her husband. Her hand swept through his head and out the other side. She yelled, "You're dead, dead!" She swiped at him again, making his hair blow in the breeze from her arm.

Scotty stood open-mouthed in amazement. Alyse understood; she, too, had spent days convinced that she was dreaming or hallucinating.

"Dead!" Lily hollered again, for emphasis. "Dead, and you belong in Hell, not here with me!"

"Now, Lily," The Preacher made calming motions with his hand. "God decides these things, not us."

"God would not send that sonuvabitch here with me!"

"Lily, please." Scotty began backing away. He looked frightened and, indeed, Lily in her wrath was scary. The Preacher stepped in between, and Alyse had to give him a little credit; that was brave.

"Now, Lily, we need to welcome this newcomer."

"THE HELL WITH THAT!"

Lily shot over the preacher's head. Scotty flung himself backward and landed on the ground. Lily landed on him and jumped up and down, managing to puff some dust up off the street. Scotty wriggled around and curled up in the fetal position, crying.

Jack stepped out into the street. He had the natural command that The Preacher lacked. "Lily, honey," he said.

She bounced a few more times, then curled up in the air. She was crying too.

"Come on, Lily, honey, come inside. Leave him out here to figure it out."

"I'll help him," said The Preacher. "You all can go back to your game." His tone grated on Alyse. The Preacher was always nice to people, trying to be helpful, but he had one eye on the sky as if he were trying to impress God with his kindness, as if he was thinking, "See, God, I'm better than these jerks. I'm so nice to them! Get me out of here, please!" He bent over Scotty and recited, "Though I walk through the valley of death, my rod and staff will comfort me." Alyse was not familiar with the Bible and she suspected that The Preacher, who was operating from memory, often got his quotes wrong.

She turned from the window as Jack and Lily re-entered the saloon.

"Well," said Jack, "if there was any booze in here, I'd say that called for a drink."

"That man better stay away from me," Lily snarled. "I almost killed him once, and I can do it again."

CHAPTER FOUR:
Lily

Then Lily told them her story. She had grown up poor in the Philippines, born after World War II when the islands were well-stocked with American soldiers who liked the dainty dark-haired girls. She and her sisters had hung around the base on Friday and Saturday nights, but not as prostitutes. No, they drank and danced, flirted and maybe kissed and cuddled, but that was it. They held out for marriage, and they got what they wanted.

The sisters all flew to America with their soldier husbands, but America turned out to be a big place. As the years went by, they rarely saw each other, each concentrating on her own life.

Lily's life was one of disappointment. Scotty drank, and then left the army. She worked in a factory, a sweatshop really, and as a waitress and a maid. Scotty got jobs and lost them and drank even more. When he got drunk, he got mean and beat her up. She got fed up with the beatings, so one night after he passed out, she tied him up with clothesline and worked him over from head to foot with a baseball bat.

"Jesus, Lily," said Jack, impressed.

She demonstrated her technique for them, swinging an imaginary bat down over and over. Lily was tiny, but mighty. "I start with his feet," she said, "and I go up to his head."

"I'm surprised you didn't kill him," Alyse said. She was impressed, too, but shocked.

"I almost killed him, but I didn't," Lily explained. "I waited until he woke up—"

"He slept through that?" asked Trey, amazed.

"No," Lily frowned, annoyed by Trey's obtuseness. "He was passed out from drinking. I waited until the next day when he woke up, and then I told him next time you beat me, I wait. I just wait. You pass out from drinking or fall asleep, and then I kill you. He never touched me again."

She smirked, swinging the imaginary baseball bat back and forth.

"And I'm sure you lived happily ever after," said Warren, grinning.

CHAPTER FIVE:

In the Evening When the Sun Goes Down

*J*ack was thinking about leaving. He knew his nickname was Traveling Jack, and it suited him. He had always been a roamer.

He didn't know what he'd done to deserve Limbo. He didn't know that he'd done anything to deserve Heaven or Hell either, so maybe Limbo was a fair assessment after all. He felt sorry for Alyse, dying at seventeen before she even got a shot at life. She should have gone to Heaven, assuming there was one. He'd been in his sixties when his heart gave out, so he didn't have anything to complain about; for better or worse, he'd lived.

Getting high and getting by was how he'd spent his time. Sometimes he was overcome with nostalgia for his former insouciant life of a couch surfer. Mostly the nostalgia came over him in the evenings. Jack didn't relate to mornings because he'd experienced so few of them—in life he'd rarely been awake before noon. But the evening . . . ah, that was another story. Starting with his high school years, evening had become the hunting time. Go out and hunt up some pot, or some acid, and stalk a girl. He had never raped anyone or banged a chick that had a steady guy. He just made passes at whatever available girls he could find and often scored. What was so bad about that? Mutual enjoyment.

Evidently he had not made the cut for Heaven, but hadn't screwed up enough for Hell either. So be it. But he'd like to smoke some pot in the evening or even smoke a cigarette. If he could do that, all in all he'd be pretty happy.

Really, his only other beef with the place was his neighbor, Emmanuel, who greeted each dawn with vocal exercises, waking Jack up as reliably as an alarm clock. He'd done some shouting and swearing at first, but had eventually given up. The vocal exercises only lasted fifteen minutes or so, then Emmanuel wandered off somewhere else to sing, leaving Jack to the luxury of returning to sleep. So things had worked out, nothing to get hassled about.

All in all, Limbo wasn't so bad.

But the sunsets got to Jack, stirred up something inside him. Jack sat on the roof of the saloon and watched the fading light. The sky turned a rosy color, tinged with a bit of orange, and the mountains looked like dark blue tissue paper. The last hawk floated in lazy circles in the sky, and shadows lengthened, purple on golden ground. In the distance the cows lowed, a sound as evocative of yearning as the wild wail of a train whistle. There was something about that last light of the evening and the long slanting shadows, the miles of darkening sagebrush and the moan of the distant cows, which made Jack want to jump in a car and just drive, drive, drive.

Warren drifted aimlessly in circles in his room in the upstairs of the saloon. He knew Lily was downstairs, and probably wanted company, but he was not in the mood. He wasn't in the mood for anyone in the village, really. He was in the mood for things the village could not provide, like conversation. Conversation about something substantive, like what the heck they were doing there.

"How come you look more alive than me?" he asked the dog. The dog was, according to Trey, a Treeing Walker Coonhound. He was a beat up old dog, with a ragged hole in one ear, rough, dirty fur, and a worn place around his neck from a too-tight collar. He had ambled into the village one day and stayed. Warren had invited the dog up to his room because he liked the dog's expressive brown eyes and droopy jowls. He called the dog "Dean" because of the resemblance to the Dean of the College of Liberal Arts where Warren taught before his death. "Can you explain it to me, Dean, why you look more alive than me, when I assume you are just as dead?"

As far as he could tell, the animals of the vicinity were not ghosts in the same way as the people. The cows cropped grass and defecated messy swirls of sticky brown feces in the sagebrush. The pigs grunted to each other in a continuous friendly prattle. Deer browsed the willows. Birds . . . the air was full of birds. But, lacking a bird book, Warren could not identify them. Admittedly, he had paid no attention to birds while alive; now he listened to them sing in the mornings. The birds, like the other animals surrounding them, seemed to go about the business of life, or rather, afterlife, contentedly. Warren envied them.

Warren had never been a pet owner, but he knew, as a matter of general knowledge, how to care for a dog. Many of his girlfriends had owned pet dogs—mostly small yappy foo-foo dogs that too often were inconveniently located on female laps just when he wanted to move in for a kiss. But Dean was no cherished apartment dog; he'd probably spent most of his life on a chain outside, ignored and neglected.

There was very little that Warren could do for Dean. He had no access to dog food, dog beds, water bowls, toys, or anything a normal dog owner would provide. All he could offer the dog was companionship and a place indoors to sleep. He let Dean out in the morning and let him back in at night. Dean disappeared each day for hours, and returned each evening with a satisfied air, as if the day had met his expectations, to sleep the dreamless sleep of the just. The arrangement was satisfactory to all parties.

Dean was, in a way, Warren's hobby. He wondered

why God had provided the humans with nothing to do all day except to get on each others' nerves and watch the animals flaunt their contentment. Was it a lesson in humility for humans who considered themselves to be God's superior creations? Could be.

The birds sang a lot better than the church attendees.

"What do you think, Dean?"

Dean rolled his eyes and exhaled a long blubbery snort.

"Yeah," said Warren. "That's about all I know about it, too."

Alyse curled into herself. She rarely slept inside the shack, preferring to be outside where she could see the stars. Most of her evenings were spent on forensic examinations of minor childhood events: why she had done certain things, what she had been feeling, what those around her had been doing.

She ran movies in her head about her life. She remembered playing in the yard in the summer, grass stains on her jeans, her mother annoyed. She remembered a play fight with her sister, hitting each other over the head with chunks of snow until they were both staggering around dizzy. She remembered riding her bike full speed down the hill and careening out into the horse pasture, hair flying, pedals whirling, bouncing on the verge of a serious accident.

She thought of the day she snagged a forbidden doughnut off the counter and got caught eating it. Her parents rarely bought junk food, and she had been told not to eat any of them. She couldn't remember why she snagged that doughnut. She couldn't even remember the act of snagging it. Her memory started with her hurried scamper up the stairs and the sound of her father's footsteps following, the dread in her stomach as she tried to cram the evidence into her mouth. She had felt guilty and scared, like a criminal. Her parents had not needed to punish her much. She'd punished herself.

She had mostly been a model little girl, well-behaved except for a tendency toward risk-taking. She had known, clear back to her earliest memories, that she was pretty. She had known that she was going to be one of life's winners, that her life would be a series of victories. That's how her parents lived, and how she had also expected to live.

She had not expected to get a brain tumor.

She had not expected to be exiled from her home, cut off by the unimaginable distance of death from the people who loved her.

Alyse curled into herself like a folded up blanket. She had no body to feel the hard wood of the floor, no skin to be chilled by night air. She had only her mind and the pain of her thoughts as company.

When she first arrived in Limbo, she'd been so achingly lonely that she'd sobbed herself to sleep every night. But no one can sustain such a high level of misery. Her sadness had been reduced to a chronic state, rather than a severe one. She'd been in the village long enough for the loneliness and shock to recede, to be replaced by boredom and depression. Often the depression led to anger, and the anger led to sneers and sarcasm.

But anger didn't protect her after dark. After dark the sadness seeped in the cracks and filled every corner of her mind and heart.

"I miss you," Alyse whispered. Sometimes she ached for her mother, sometimes her father, sometimes for the lost companionship of her sister. Sometimes she ached for all of them at once. She had been amputated from her family. She felt raw, bloody, and incomplete without them.

Alyse whispered, as if she were phoning home from a strange vacation, "I went to the river today. I went wading in the river. I went flying, too, with one of my neighbors."

She tried to imagine introducing her parents and her sister to Trey. They would be polite, but distant. He would be shy. "It's different here," she told her family. "You will come here, too, someday." But probably not her part of Limbo. That's what the others said: you didn't get to reunite with loved ones. You only got stuck with people you had hated or with strangers. Another dirty trick from God.

She would never see her family again. Alyse curled into a tight little ball and cried herself to sleep.

CHAPTER SIX:
Scotty is Dead

Alyse and Trey sat on her front steps and watched Scotty staggering up the road. He still tried to walk on the dirt as if his body had weight. Some of his steps sank deep into the ground, and sometimes he over-compensated and shot up in the air, flapping his arms for balance.

He looked terrible—darkness around his eyes, face streaked with the memory of rain, toothless mouth hanging open. Trey called out, "Hey, Scotty."

Scotty stopped. He hung in the air, swaying.

"How you doing, man?" Trey asked.

"I dunno." He tried to rub his eyes and stuck his fist into his face. "I dunno. I just can't get used to it, I guess."

"Being dead?"

"Yeah," Scotty revolved slowly in a circle. "Hey, is there any other saloon besides Lily's?"

"No. There's no liquor either." Trey spoke with

sympathy, though he had never been much of a drinker.

"No liquor?" That got Scotty's attention. "None at all?"

"No, man. Sorry to break the news."

"This town is dry?" Scotty squeaked with dismay.

"Hey," Alyse cut in. "We're ghosts. We don't eat or drink anything. We don't poop, we don't take baths or change our clothes or comb our hair or do anything we used to do."

She thought, but did not say, we don't have sex either.

Scott stared at her, mouth ajar.

Alyse leaned forward for emphasis, "We are ghosts." She sat back.

Trey gave her a sideways look and whispered, "He's probably detoxing."

"I . . ." Scotty twisted around, looking up the street and down. He was at a loss.

"Y'all can come up here and sit with us," Trey invited.

They moved over to make room. Alyse thought it was a good thing Scotty was a ghost because otherwise he would have been pretty disgusting. It was obvious that in life he had been dirty. It was hard to imagine Lily putting up with him, even for the occasional paycheck.

They just sat quietly for a while. Then Scotty asked, "Is this your house, Trey?"

"No, this is Alyse's place. I sleep over at the other end."

"I got no place to sleep," Scotty whined. Alyse thought, Scotty's going to give Trey competition for sad, old dog status around here.

"You can share with me, if you haven't found a place yet," Trey suggested.

So two sad old dogs rooming together. Alyse hated the thought of sharing with anyone. She wanted a place all her own.

"Thanks, man," said Scotty. He was shaking. Alyse could feel the shivers running up and down his torso.

"I'm trying," Scotty moaned. He rocked back and forth. "I'm trying to get used to it."

CHAPTER SEVEN:
Church

Lily could not find God in The Preacher's church. It was a bare brown building, just one room with unpainted walls. No stained glass. In fact, the windows lacked any glass at all. Only the steeple indicated that the building was a church.

No choir, no pulpit, no candles, no wafer, no incense, no Latin liturgy. No priest.

Lily was the only parishioner who knelt on the hard, dirty floor. The rest of the congregation sat, floated or leaned up against the wall. They stayed away from the ceiling in order to give some contrast to The Preacher who floated a few feet over their heads.

The Preacher wore no vestments, just a shapeless, gray hospital gown.

His preaching didn't help Lily feel any closer to God. He was talking about lifting one's eyes to the hills from whence cometh strength. Lily had never thought of the outdoors having much to do with religion. She didn't like preaching in English, either. She liked a Latin mass, the incomprehensible mysterious drone that invited her heart to feel the inexpressible. This sermon was just some guy talking. Lily clasped her hands in prayer and closed her eyes. It didn't help.

Alyse looked out the window toward the distant mountains and thought about strength. She didn't have any. She wanted to shout and hit and bite. She wanted to cry all the time.

The Preacher said that the Bible text meant that people were to lift their eyes beyond human affairs, above the sinfulness of people and their bad works, and instead, think of the purity of Heaven and the forgiveness of God.

When God forgave them, they would go to Heaven, he said. He rolled his eyes upward, toward the dry grey wood of the ceiling.

Lily thought, why did God forgive Scotty and keep him out of Hell? Why is God punishing me by putting him here?

Alyse thought, what did I do that was so bad? She hadn't had time to be a big sinner. She hadn't had a chance to live at all.

Afterwards, back at her shack, her place of exile, Alyse thought about the church service. The part about sinners and God's forgiveness made her chest tighten up with distress. It seemed wrong. If God had to forgive them, then there was something wrong with them, and why had God, who created them, make them fundamentally wrong? Maybe they were supposed to forgive God.

Back at the saloon, Lily went down on her knees. She had no candles, incense, no priest, no rosary, no singing, no cross, but also no idiot preacher interrupting her thoughts with his babbling.

She tried to feel God.

All she felt was outrage. Why was Scotty there and not in Hell? Why was she being punished when he was the sinner? She tried to pray, but could find no words that were not accusatory. She felt as if she was on the brink of a terrifying doubt, about to believe something she should not allow herself to contemplate.

Why had God sent her Scotty and not a priest?

CHAPTER EIGHT:
Round Two

Having Scotty and Lily show up in the same town was the best entertainment the community had had in—well, since no one could keep track of time, no one knew how long. But relatives and friends and enemies from life were rare. The villagers were an odd mixed lot, mostly middle-aged or old people, mostly English speakers, but some not. As far as they could tell, they were a random selection of dead people who were not good enough for Heaven or bad enough for Hell.

The main thing they had in common was their clothes; many wore hospital gowns because they had died while hospitalized. The lack of appropriate clothing caused some embarrassment. Trey's gown didn't cover his large butt with its strange geography of bed sore canyons. Lily was determined to keep anyone from seeing her tiny tail hanging out of her flapping gown. The Preacher had to do his preaching barefoot and in his hospital draperies.

And then there was The Naked Man. He had suddenly appeared in the village, completely bereft of cover, to his intense embarrassment and the amusement of those villagers who observed his arrival. It was Warren who told the newcomer that there were empty rooms in the saloon. The Naked Man sprinted up the stairs where he'd remained in hiding ever since, too shy to come back down.

Alyse was one of the better dressed. She'd died in a pair of flannel PJs, red with white flowers, with a quilted bed jacket draped over her shoulders. Scotty had died of hyperthermia in soiled jeans, a torn T-shirt, and old trainers. Even after death, he looked wet.

The town put Alyse in mind of a movie set haunted by mental patients. She was glad to be one of the better-dressed ones. Gathered into a group, they were a sight to behold.

And gathered they were one afternoon, because Lily and Scotty were fighting again.

It started during a poker game. Lily had been dealing as usual. She tossed the cards like a pro, skimming them through the air to land face down in front of each player.

"Y'all ante up now."

Sometimes they affected accents to make the game jollier.

"Ooo my, lookee here," said Jack, grinning wolfishly at his hole cards. They pitched in their antes.

"And here's another, down and dirty." Lily slapped the last round down.

"Well, grassy-ass, senioreeter," Jack drawled, after

picking up his last card. "I'm gonna raise you all two rocks and a stick."

That's when Scotty wafted in.

Lily went rigid.

"Sorry, don't mind me," said Scotty, hunching into himself apologetically. "I'll just watch. I don't need to play."

"What makes you think you can come into my house?" Lily's voice started out low, but got louder and louder until her last words came out in a shriek. She rose to her feet and continued the rise up into the air. Scotty backed up until he was halfway through the wall.

"Lily, I just wanted to watch, that's all."

"Hey, Lily," Jack said, "C'mon, let's play. Let the man watch."

"NOT IN MY HOUSE!" Lily screamed. She made a swoosh through the air, and the wallpaper cards went flying. Jack tried to slap down his cards, but his hand went right through the floor. Trey struggled upward, like a huge balloon. Alyse and Warren melted into the wall to watch.

Lily had prepared for this day with a stick. No one had noticed it propped up against the wall. She wrapped her fingers around it—not a grab, just a careful solidifying of her palm so as to get a grip—and lifted the stick. Scotty whined, "Lily, please," and retreated through the wall.

Lily shot through the wall after him, but the stick could not follow. She lost her grip and entered the street in a series of undignified somersaults. Recovering herself, she yelled with frustration, re-entered through the open door, and retrieved her stick. As she flew out into the street, the other ghosts followed her. Scotty was hovering outside, looking uncomfortable and embarrassed.

Lily lifted the stick like a baseball bat. She and Scotty hovered about twenty feet apart in the middle of the dirt road. Alyse joined Trey, Jack, and Warren in front of the saloon to watch the shoot-out. Alyse didn't know what to think, didn't know if the spectacle was amusing or appalling. Or both. Warren grinned sardonically, but Trey just looked sad.

Jack was pissed that his winning hand had been spoiled.

"Hey, Lily, you can't beat up an unarmed man!" he hollered.

Lily glared at him. "Then find him a stick," she challenged Jack. "And hurry."

"I don't want a stick," Scotty whimpered. "I don't want to fight."

Other people were gathering. Across the street Darla and The Chinese Lady appeared along with some other adults that Alyse recognized as church choir singers, but didn't know by name.

"It ain't a fight if Scotty can't fight back," Jack jeered. "Come on Lily, fight fair! Give Scotty a stick!"

He thinks this is funny, Alyse thought. She exchanged glances with Trey.

"Lily, I'm sorry," Scotty whispered.

"You no good!" In her excitement Lily seemed to be losing her English. "No good!" She took a swipe at the air with her stick.

Scotty cringed backwards a few feet. "I know, Lily. I never was any good."

"You bring me to America. Big talk. No good!" She darted forward, and Scotty dodged backwards.

"I know," he whined. "I'm sorry."

As Lily advanced, Scotty retreated. They moved down the street far enough that the poker players no longer had ringside seats. Jack yelled, "Are you gonna to hit him or what? If you ain't, come back so we can finish the game."

"I don't want to play anymore," Alyse whispered to Trey.

"No good!" Lily continued to yell. "Stay away!" She flung the stick down in the dirt.

The show was over.

Lily steamed back into the saloon, her long hair flying behind her. Jack followed, but stopped in the door and looked back at Trey, Alyse, and Warren. "You guys coming?"

"Sure," said Warren.

"Yeah, OK," said Trey.

"I'm going home," said Alyse.

CHAPTER NINE:
Looking for God

Lily longed for a candle. She knelt in the closet at the back of the saloon, a storage room with no windows, just dust and spider webs and a rusted tin can. The wind blew through the cracks in the wood. She knelt on the floor, making her legs as substantial as she could. She wanted to feel the pain of flesh against solid wood. She bent forward, her head dangling over her lap, her hair hiding her face, her hands clasped.

"Father, forgive me . . ."

Her whisper dried out, wafted away by the thin cold wind that hissed through the walls.

She yearned for a candle. The light would help her, she believed. A warm yellow light, a beacon, a gateway, an aspiration. Something to look at besides the dingy dried-out grayish brown of the walls, the buildings, the streets, the town.

Her eyes ached with unshed tears. "Please, Father."

She tried again, "Please, Father, why have you

abandoned me?"

She had gone to Mass weekly. She had prayed daily before meals, even when Scotty mocked her. She had allowed Scotty to have sex with her, even though she hadn't liked it, and she had never used birth control. God had denied them children, and she had always wondered why. Now she thought that the lack of children was probably the first of her punishments for her sins, whatever those sins were.

She couldn't think of any sins out of the ordinary. She had gone to confession regularly. She had tried her best, but her best had never been good enough. Now she didn't have a priest, could not confess, could not attend Mass, could not speak to God and tell Him what was in her heart.

She leaned forward, then slowly lay herself on the floor of the storage room. She curled up in the fetal position. Her face ached, her chest hurt. She felt a black hole of emptiness inside where belief used to reside. "Please," she begged. "Please."

Warren decided to follow Dean out into the sagebrush, but he couldn't keep up. Dean knew he was following. He looked back a few times, but didn't slow his long loping strides. There were no pathways. Dean swerved easily between the sagebrush scrubs, his relaxed strides eating up distance until Warren could see only his tail and then lost him altogether.

Warren kept walking. He couldn't get lost. The plain

rose gently toward the mountains, and the buildings of the town, a ragged row of brown angles and lines, were visible for miles. He just kept drifting onward and upward for lack of anything else to do.

Maybe he didn't really want to see Dean kill and eat anything anyway, if that's what Dean did out there. He could imagine the pain and fear of Dean's prey. It affected his attitude toward Dean; there was obviously more to the dog than his morose expression and loud slobbery snores.

Dean was intelligent and conniving; he could track, pursue, and possibly kill. Warren felt bad now about all of the animals he had eaten when alive. Not that he had hunted them anywhere except the grocery store or restaurant. But he had eaten meat with no particular thought about where it came from or that the meat had once been an animal who didn't want to die. Now that he didn't need to eat, he did ponder it, and he had come to the conclusion that he should have been a vegetarian.

While he mused, he slogged along. Movement as a ghost didn't require much effort. In fact, sometimes the effort went into not moving; it was possible to be blown away on windy days. Today wasn't windy. In the stillness of the air, he could feel vague warmth from the sun. Along with it came lethargy, a desire to lie in the dirt and soak up the sun.

Warren found a small open area of dirt and dry grass between the ubiquitous sagebrush and plopped down.

He expected to get bored. Seated on the ground, he could no longer see over the bushes to the town. All he could see was the shrubbery around him. Tiny, stiff, dry, grayish green leaves, all alike.

Except they weren't. Close examination revealed that each leaf was unique within a similar elongated oval shape. They stuck out from the skinny branches in a non-repeating pattern. The word "fractal" came to mind, but math, especially higher math, had not been his area of study. The leaves appeared to attach to the branch in the same way, but in reality the overall pattern was one of variation.

Warren reached out for a twig. He tried to break the twig off, but could not give his fingers enough substance to get a good grip. He succeeded only in bending the twig so that it hung by threads of xylem.

He studied the broken twig hanging from the injured bush. He had wanted the twig for his room, but all he had done was create ugliness, incongruence, a break in the pattern of the bush's growth.

He tried not to see significance in that. Every single thing was not weighty, he told himself. When he looked back on his life, that's what he observed: a man who had spent every minute treating every minor decision as if it was hugely important, while frequently missing the real issues.

As a student of literature, he had been very aware of how the details of daily life indicated character, and while he had agreed with the ancient Greek notion that character was largely a determiner of fate, he had valued the details too highly. He had been overly concerned that his fate should involve a tasteful condo, corduroy jackets, hair cut just long enough to imply careless rebellion, frequent dates with attractive women, tenure (of course), and maybe eventually a deanship.

All of that ambition had turned to dust and sagebrush, an eternity in a hospital gown.

Alyse and Trey sat together on her front steps. It occurred to her that it was strange for a teenager to have a fortyish man for a friend. A seventy-year-old man would be acceptable, because that would signify a grandfatherly type of relationship. A twenty-five-year-old man would be OK for a budding romance—a little old for a seventeen-year-old girl, but not too weird. Her parents would never have allowed her to date anyone that age, but her parents were not in the village, and anyway she was not dating Trey. They were just friends.

She was buddies with a forty-year-old quadriplegic.

She wanted to ask her friend about sex. What was it really like? He had been married; he had a ring. But she didn't feel she was good enough friends with him to approach that topic directly. So she asked, "Trey, what were you like when you were my age?"

There was a long silence. She was getting used to Trey's slow answers. "I was on the football team. I guess I was pretty good, because they didn't want me to quit."

"Didn't you like being on the team?" That amazed her. She had loved being on the track team. All of her friends had been on teams of some sort, even if the team was choir or band.

"Yeah, I liked playing football." Trey let his gaze wander to the past. He was watching himself in high school, seeing himself walking down a dusty Texas road in a landscape not too different from Limbo, a heavy, clumsy young man with a shy smile and eyes that never saw too far ahead.

"I dropped out of school, but the principal came out to my house and talked to my mom and dad, and they all pushed me into going back. They gave me passing grades to keep me in school, so I could play on the team."

"Really?" So much of Trey's life was beyond her ken. Decent grades were required for team membership in her school, but none of the girls had ever been in danger of being less than a B student. She didn't know anyone who flunked out or dropped out. "They must have really wanted you on the team."

"I guess they did." He didn't seem particularly proud, which puzzled Alyse. She didn't realize that in Trey's small hometown every player was important.

She tried a different topic, "Did you go to dances and parties when you were in high school?"

That lit Trey up. "Yeah, me and my friend Duane, we even crashed a party this one time."

He told her the story. Duane was wild. He'd dropped out of school because he had a business selling drugs, pot mostly, but also meth. He had a Mustang that he'd rebuilt, painted, polished, and kept in his mother's garage.

The interior was always immaculate. He kept a blanket in the backseat. Trey had assumed the blanket was for sex, because he thought Duane was way ahead of him in that department, but in reality the blanket was to protect Duane's passenger seat from desecration by any passengers. He didn't want anyone's blue jeans touching his upholstery.

He didn't allow smoking in his car, either, even though he smoked like a chimney. That was Trey's memory of Duane: jeans, black ZZ Top T-shirt, baseball cap and brash cigarette, leaning on his beautifully polished car. Duane had been all muscle and bone when young. Hip. He'd become leathery and pot-bellied with age, but as a young man he had been as feral and tough as a cougar, the cigarette as much a part of his mouth as his tongue.

It was the cigarette that caused them to crash the party. Because of Duane's nicotine addiction, when he and Trey went out on Saturday nights they always took Trey's vehicle, a derelict and dilapidated Chevy pickup.

They did what all the boys did on Saturday nights. They cruised up the main drag, turned around, and drove back down again. They bought a six pack and cigarettes. Duane was older, so getting the beer wasn't usually a problem. They drank and smoked, snorted some meth, and toked some pot. Trouble called, mostly in the form of posturing with other truckloads of guys they knew but didn't always like from high school. Sometimes there were fights, but mostly it was just lots of shouting and screeching of tires.

Looking back, Trey didn't remember much girl-hunting going on, but at the time he'd had the impression that Duane was getting all he wanted. Trey wasn't. Trey was big, block-shaped, slow, and shy. He looked at girls, but wouldn't talk to them.

They were out cruising one hot Texas night, smoking and drinking and getting high, yelling at the guys they knew and revving the engine of the old truck at the guys they didn't know, when this kid from school told them about the party.

The party was on Rio Verde Street, which said everything that needed to be said in Trey's hometown. It meant snobs, kids whose parents were in management, not kids like Trey who had parents who worked the line, or were in one of the trades. Rio Verde was in a development of McMansions on streets that were all Rio This or That. There was no actual river anywhere in the vicinity.

So he and Duane and the truckload of other kids decided to crash the party they hadn't been invited to. Trey hadn't really intended anything more than a drive-by, some honking, and maybe a beer can tossed on the lawn. But they'd all been pretty high.

So they went careening out onto the highway toward the development, both trucks driving too fast because the other was egging them on. Trey drove. Duane stuck his head out the window and hollered into the darkness, shaking his fist in the air like people do when their team scores a goal.

Trey almost missed the corner into the development. He spun the wheel and wrangled the truck around the corner, up onto the sidewalk, back down to the black top, and got them aimed down the street without hitting one of the newly-planted trees. Duane whooped his approval. Trey thought, "I'm drunk"—but sometimes you just don't care.

He swung the wheel back and forth, zigzagging for no reason except to make Duane shout louder. The other truck zigzagged, too, honking.

Trey didn't know where Rio Verde Street was, and neither did anyone else. They drove too fast to read the street signs. They just rocketed around being obnoxious, when suddenly the party came into view.

It was an outdoor party, with colored lights, pop music, and twenty or so kids outside drinking sodas and beer while parents watched from the front porch. Trey had been zigging and zagging and the unexpected sight of the party caused him to make an especially sharp zig. Suddenly his truck was rolling up the sidewalk and toward the lawn party.

It was like the truck was driving itself while Trey watched with horror. The tone of Duane's yelling changed to shrill bleats of alarm. The other truck was still right behind him, just a yard off Trey's bumper.

Trey didn't even think of his brakes. He thought only of his steering wheel. He zagged toward the street, but was hemmed in by parked cars. Trey zigged back toward the houses. He had the vague impression of kids flying in all directions. A card table flew up into the air. Colored lights flashed by. Trey finally remembered to brake, just before the truck slammed to an abrupt halt against the side of the house. There was a second shock when the following truck hit Trey's back bumper.

Trey extricated himself from behind the steering wheel. There was no airbag. His chest felt like he'd been kicked by a horse, and his nose was bleeding. He turned to Duane, but Duane was already halfway out the window. Duane landed headfirst on the lawn, staggered to his feet, and ran.

Trey had known there was no point to running. He just sat and waited for the police.

"So that's how I crashed a party," he told Alyse, smiling a little at the memory. "I coulda died, but I guess that wasn't the plan."

"So what happened?" she asked. "Did you get in trouble?" She was thinking that she was like the party kids. If she and Trey had been the same age at the same school, they would not have been friends.

"Oh, I got arrested, but my parents bailed me out. I didn't get in much trouble because it was football season."

Wow, Alyse thought, I never did anything like that.

Now she never would.

CHAPTER TEN:
The Naked Man is Missing

The Chinese Lady stood in the middle of the street, pointing and jabbering. Since there was nothing else going on, she had drawn a small crowd. Warren stood beside her, trying to figure out what she was yelling about. She was pointing at the upstairs window of the saloon.

"There's nothing up there." Warren tried to show patience with The Chinese Lady.

"Ou oiu." She pointed urgently, stabbing the air with her finger. Her words were round, lots of "O" sounds, as if she had an apple in her mouth.

There was nothing in the window. Just a blank darkness. Then Warren figured it out. No Naked Man. He was often seen in the window, looking out at the street.

"Oh, I get it."

Warren went into the saloon. He expected to find Lily there, but the big, dark room was empty. "Lily," he called.

The bare walls answered him with silence. "Lily, you here?" he yelled.

"What!" Lily erupted through the wall of the storage closet. Warren wondered briefly what she had been doing in the closet, but he didn't really care. She looked annoyed, but that was normal.

"I just wondered if you had seen The Naked Man lately."

"I never see him since he got here. He went up there, and he stayed up there."

"Oh. I wonder if he's still up there."

Lily shrugged. Warren hesitated. It wasn't his business. Still it was weird. Maybe The Naked Man was gone. There were implications to that which interested Warren. He floated up the stairs with Lily following, grumbling, "I'm not his landlady. He don't pay no rent."

They stopped outside the closed door and hung in the air, irresolute, intimidated by the silence. They both felt hesitant about busting through into The Naked Man's private space. Warren hardened up his knuckles and knocked. The sound was tiny, just a dry rustle. No response.

Warren cleared his throat and called softly, "Are you at home?" He thought about asking, "Are you decent?" but it seemed a poor joke.

No one answered.

"Maybe he's gone," Lily said.

"Should we go in to check?" Warren asked. Lily shrugged. Warren fidgeted, thinking about the implications of checking versus not checking. He made up his mind and stuck his head through the door.

The room was empty.

"No one's there."

They both eased through the door cautiously. The room was barren, just a brown featureless box. Viewed from the inside, the window was a glare of light. A patch of yellow sunlight illuminated the dust on the floor. The Naked Man had left no indication that he had ever occupied the dreary, silent space.

"Jesus," Warren whispered, "I wonder where he went."

Lily guffawed, "He's out in the sagebrush somewhere. Out there with his johnson. I'm glad he's gone."

"I don't know," said Warren. He felt disturbed by the absence of The Naked Man. He had only been in the village a little while and now, suddenly, he was gone.

The news got to Trey by way of the town crier, Darla. A tall, striking woman of great certainty, she had situated herself in the middle building on the main road, the better to involve herself in all village affairs. Alyse didn't like her; Darla was too much on the model of PTA moms, the sort of woman who was in the foreground of all school events. Alyse wasn't sure why she didn't like Darla, since her own mother was of that type. Maybe it was the frenetic need to be busy when there was nothing to be busy about.

"Darla says The Naked Man has gone on."

"Going on" could mean just heading down the road as

Jack had done many times, or it could mean something far more significant. Hope had bred conviction; most of the villagers believed that there was another afterlife somewhere beyond Limbo, somewhere else for the dead to go, somewhere better. There was no consensus on how to get to this better place. The Preacher believed in a traditional Heaven reached by prayer for forgiveness of sin. His afterlife was a place of cloud and harmony and eternal kneeling before the altar of God. Alyse could not imagine what change it would take in the human mind, short of a lobotomy, to make such an existence tolerable.

"I don't know why The Naked Man would go to Heaven," she said, hoping that Trey would not respond with a platitude about the will of God.

He didn't. "I just hope he's happier wherever he is."

It occurred to Alyse that The Naked Man might be hiding out in the sagebrush, friendless and alone. He had been friendless and alone in town, too, of course. She had never thought of befriending him. It creeped her out to think of being around a naked adult male.

But now she felt desolate. They should have done something for him, or at least tried.

CHAPTER ELEVEN:
Sometimes You're Better Off Dead

Trey and Alyse got into the habit of sitting together while Trey told stories of his life. He had lots of stories. One day he told her how he died.

"I guess I just thought you died of being paralyzed," she said.

"No, people can go on for years now," he explained. "I took a lot of morphine for the pain, but I could have lived for . . . I don't know, years. I died because my caregiver gave me a drug overdose."

Alyse was shocked. "How could anyone do that? If someone is supposed to care for you . . . did she go to jail?"

"Go to jail? No, nothing like that. It was an accident. She gave me my morphine twice, and then it went toxic on me. I kind of went into a, like a dream state, and then I died, and she didn't notice because she was asleep, too."

"My God, Trey, that's awful," Alyse was indignant.

"She killed you!"

"Well, I guess she did, but she had troubles of her own."

"But she was supposed to be caring for you. It was her job."

"We shouldn't have hired her. I knew she had troubles. She was my step-daughter." Trey shifted position, so he could see farther out over the dry grass and the distant expanse of prairie. He was looking back to Texas, toward a small town in cotton country.

"The state paid her, so the money went to care for my grandchildren. I knew we were asking too much of her, but I wanted the money for the kids."

"Trey! That's not OK." Alyse couldn't understand why he wasn't angry.

"I helped raise her." Trey shrugged his shoulders. "Her mother and me, I guess we didn't do a very good job. She was always troubled."

He'd gotten married right out of high school to a girl who already had a baby, the step-daughter who killed him. Then Trey and his wife had two more kids. Donna, the step-daughter, had grown up unmanageable and had gotten pregnant four times before she was twenty-two. Trey had loved the grandkids—they'd given meaning to his life.

Alyse contemplated Trey's life: an early marriage, all those kids right out of high school, trying to be a father. She could not imagine him being a disciplinarian with the kids. He was the kind of guy who would love the kids the way a dog loves, without making any demands, as close to unconditional as one can get. She wondered if there had been much love between him and his wife, or if she just married him because she needed help supporting her child.

"How did you get hurt?" She was trying to imagine how a quadriplegic could have children.

"I got hurt at work. I drove a forklift, and a bunch of oil barrels fell on top of me. The forklift has this roof, to protect you if stuff falls, but when the barrels came down, they knocked me out of the forklift. We sued, but the settlement wasn't that much, and the lawyers got the lion's share of it."

Trey sighed and gazed out into the warm air of morning. The conversation was making him feel sad. "Anyway . . . that's what happened. I'm not sorry to be dead. I just miss the kids."

"I'm sorry I asked, Trey," Alyse apologized.

Trey shrugged again. "I was on so much morphine that it was almost like being dead anyway." He paused, thinking. "I know I shouldn't be glad to be dead because the Bible says that we are supposed to be grateful for life and not take life, including our own. But the only thing I am sad about is leaving the kids and never seeing them again."

"Oh, well," he added, "Now they get my Social Security check, so that's something. I just wish I knew if they were OK."

Alyse wanted to tell Trey stories about her life, but compared to him, she didn't have any. She had not wrecked a car or gotten drunk or skipped school, and she certainly had not gotten married. She had been kissed a couple times, once by a guy she didn't like.

That was a story.

"I punched a guy in the nose once and made it bleed," Alyse said.

Trey grinned, "Good for you!"

"It happened after a school dance. I went to the dance with another girl because neither of us was dating anyone." Alyse glanced defensively at Trey, wondering if he thought she couldn't get dates. She could, but she'd been choosy. "Anyway, she drove her car and we went as singles and had a lot of fun—danced with a ton of guys—then it got really late. We went out to her car to go home, but it wouldn't start."

Alyse paused for dramatic effect. Trey said, "If all those guys were still around, someone should have fixed your car."

"Well, there were a lot of guys around, and this one guy that my friend Taylor knew was walking by, so she asked him for help. He said he'd give us a ride home. So we went to his car, and when we got there Taylor got in the back seat, which I thought was weird since he was her friend, but I didn't say anything and just got in the front. Our high school was on the edge of town out in this new neighborhood with new houses. Anyway, he drove right past my street and out of town. And I started asking what are you doing, where are you going, and so did Taylor, and he didn't even look at us or answer."

"What an asshole. I know what he had in mind," Trey growled.

Surprised at Trey's protectiveness, Alyse continued her story, "Well, he suddenly pulled over into this grove of trees by a farmhouse that looked spooky and abandoned. And then he turned to me and tried to kiss me."

Alyse found herself feeling embarrassed. "So I hauled off and punched him in the nose," she finished in a rush.

Trey laughed.

"And Taylor was yelling 'Let me out, let me out of the back seat', but I said no. I told him to drive us back to town, or I would hit him again."

"Good for you!" Trey grinned with approval. "Good girl!"

"Anyway, that was my big adventure, I guess." She and Trey exchanged smiles of comradery. She felt bad, though. Her story was about being assertive, in control, while Trey's story was of drifting into situations he couldn't manage.

That night, when Alyse curled up to sleep, she thought, as she always did, of her parents and her sister. She thought of them going on with their lives. Andee was probably dating, studying, and painting, at least Alyse hoped she was. Her parents would be home, as they almost always were in the evenings, her dad in his chair perusing work-related tomes, the lamp burning on the end table. Her mother would be at the dining room table, going over papers of her own, dry stuff having something to do with city government. The TV would be on as background noise, no one watching or listening, playing some nature program or history—they were TV snobs, after all.

Were they thinking of her? Did they miss her?

Or was she forgotten?

She pictured them staring off into space, her dad looking past his book, her mom gazing out over her papers. Remembering her.

"Please remember me," she whispered. "Please miss me."

She should be upstairs in bed with a book. She should be able to hear the soft chatter of the TV, hear her dad make a comment and a brief response from her mom. She should be able to hear the quiet sounds of her home, the hum of the furnace, the padding of cat feet in the hall, the sigh of wind around the roof. She thought of the gift her family had given her: the strength to manage her own life.

Then God or fate or chance or whatever had taken that life from her. Loss of life. The phrase popped into her head. It was a standard phrase used by TV newscasters, one she'd never considered much: loss of life in battle, loss of life in a storm.

Now her life was lost. Her life was gone, irretrievable for no valid reason. Her yearning for her life was like a sickness, an all-consuming ache, a need too deep for tears. She rolled into a little ball with her hands pressed into her face.

CHAPTER TWELVE:

Dean Finds The Naked Man

Dean was on the hunt. His long gangly legs ate up miles, loping around, over, and through the brush, relentless as a heat-seeking missile. He moved through a world of scent; easily, rapidly processing incoming information, immediately shifting his course in response to data. His tracking system was honed in on the scent of a rabbit.

The rabbit dodged around the sage, left, right, left. It ran in spurts, then hid, listening. At the sound of Dean's heavy breathing, which the rabbit could hear long before Dean came into sight, the rabbit bolted again. It was getting tired, desperate.

Dean's legs powered through the brush at an unhurried lope. He would sprint when the rabbit came into view. He knew he was closing in.

Dean's focus on the scent trail was so complete that he nearly ran right through the ghost.

The ghost was sitting in the dirt. Dean skidded to a

halt, and thoughts of the rabbit jumped right out of his mind, replaced by his ingrained response to human ghosts. This was not *his* human ghost, but that didn't matter. He stopped anyway. Dog and ghost gazed at each other in surprise.

"Well, hi there," said the ghost. The ghost was a skinny old man, stooped, his arms and legs stringy with thin muscles that barely covered his bones. He was naked, not that Dean noticed. Dean noticed his kind, quiet voice.

The old man touched Dean lightly on the head. Dean leaned into his fingers, and the man responded by scratching behind Dean's ears. Dean liked to be scratched, but wished the ghosts would do it harder, really dig in, which they never did.

He didn't know they couldn't.

"So what are you doing out here?" the old man asked.

Dean didn't answer. He'd started thinking about rabbits again. He loved to chase rabbits. He'd spent years as a chained-up backyard dog, but now that he was dead, he could spend his time doing what he loved the most—chasing rabbits until he was exhausted, and sleeping at home with his human.

The old man patted his head again.

"I wish you could talk," he said. "We have something in common—we're both naked." The man laughed a little.

Dean sniffed. He could scent the sage, the dirt, the far off cottonwood grove, the water of the river hidden by the trees, the cow poop, a deer mouse . . .

"You got business to attend to?" The Naked Man

asked. "Got places to go, things to do?"

Dean did have places to go and things to do. The rabbit scent was still in the air, though dissipated by the light breeze and mixed with other odors. He had to pick the scent up and get going again, or he would miss his chance and have to start over with a different scent trail.

"That's OK," said The Naked Man. "You go on. I'll see you another time."

Dean gave a little woof and trotted off into the bushes, nose down. In a moment he was gone, and the ghost went right out of his thoughts.

CHAPTER THIRTEEN:
Mahdi

He wasn't much taller than a sagebrush shrub. He was very thin, had large eyes, a wide forehead and a prominent nose. He wore jeans, a t-shirt, and a lifejacket, all wet. His last memory of life was of drowning.

His family had crowded onto a boat with thirty or forty other people, jammed in with their knees in each other's backs. The boat's little engine had struggled to push the boat up and down the waves. Out on the water, out of sight of land, mashed in with his family and the other terrified refugees, he'd yearned for the hard, solid dryness of the desert.

Now, suddenly, he was surrounded by dust and brushy plants under a sunny sky. He was confused.

He had a memory of falling beneath the waves. The boat tipped, spilling people into the water, and the heavy waves threw people every which way. He'd screamed for his mother, but his mouth filled with water, and his vision went from blue to gray to black. Then he'd appeared here, out in the middle of a wide prairie surrounded by scrubby bushes.

His wish to feel the hard dry land of a desert had been granted. But he was not home. It was not the desert he remembered. The bushes were different. The skyline was different. And where was his mother? His father? Where was he?

The thought of his parents galvanized him into action. He called out shrilly, crying for his parents, but his voice was only a thin wisp that evaporated in the vast expanse of prairie. He screamed again, trying for volume, but the only answer he got was the blue silence of the sky and the dry swish of wind through the brush. He was just as lost and isolated on the prairie as he had been while tossed on the waves.

He tried to run, but his body wafted upwards, got caught by a breeze, and got hung up on a bush. To his horror, he could see right through his flesh; he had turned into a grayish rag, a scrap of life, a wisp of thickened air. That's when he realized that he was either dead or dreaming.

He tried to wake himself up by slapping himself in the face, but his hand just flew in one side of his head and out the other. He shook himself. He shouted and cried. Nothing worked; he could not wake from the nightmare.

Mahdi knelt and prayed. He prayed all day and through the night. Finally, he thought he heard the voice of Allah, and he knew he was dead. He was only ten years old.

The next day he woke to find himself curled under sagebrush like a baby antelope. He carefully emerged, realized that he was still dead, and accepted that he was a ghost. His only hope was that his parents and brothers and sisters were ghosts, too, and they were nearby. He set off to look for them.

He quickly learned how to move without getting blown off course by the wind. He more or less walked, feet skimming the ground, moving around the sagebrush bushes rather than through them because he did not like being a ghost. He headed down slope, rather than toward the mountains. He passed The Naked Man, but did not see him.

The Naked Man saw the boy and hid. He didn't want to be mistaken for a flasher.

Dean spotted the ghost boy and broke off his rabbit hunt. He watched the child's hesitant wafting movements. He could tell that the little boy had no destination in mind, no idea where he should be going.

A new ghost was more interesting than a rabbit. Dean abandoned his rabbit hunting without a thought. He trotted up to the boy and woofed a friendly greeting.

The boy danced sideways, startled and fearful. He and the lanky hound were nearly the same size, and the boy's first thought was that the dog might attack him, bite him right in the face.

But Dean simply stood and watched the boy, head cocked. They stared at each other in mutual confusion.

Dean could not understand why the boy was afraid, and the boy did not understand what Dean wanted. Mahdi had seen dogs before: skinny, mangy street dogs with their hungry eyes, their backs hunched over as if they were ashamed of their very existence.

This dog had a beat-up appearance, but stood straight, looked him in the eye, and drooled. The drool—what did that mean? A disease? Then suddenly the dog smiled. There was no other word for it. His sloppy mouth opened in an ear-to-ear grin, and he woofed again, emitting a hot blast of smelly dog breath.

The boy was the second ghost to interrupt Dean's rabbit chasing that day, but Dean didn't mind. Dean liked ghosts. He decided to head back home and take the boy with him. He gave a whine to get the boy's attention, then began to walk in the direction of the village.

After a few yards, he looked back. Good, the boy followed. Dean led the way down the long slope of prairie toward the shacks, the boy trailing along behind.

The boy saw the line of roofs and realized that the dog had led him to a community. He didn't know if that was good or bad. It could be a village of people who would be terrified of him, a ghost. Or it could be a village of djinn or witches and things could get even worse for him—he no longer knew what was true and what was fantasy.

So he crept carefully through the brush, and angled toward the edge of town, moving closer and closer, silently. The hound dog approached the town more confidently. They both stopped at the sight of The Chinese Lady sitting on her back steps. She was a ghost, too.

The boy and the dog watched her whisper and sing to the cats and the plants. She seemed kind.

CHAPTER FOURTEEN:
The Chinese Lady

Ay Ling was putzing around in the backyard when she heard a woof from the prairie and saw the ghost child and the hound dog.

She had been a prolific gardener in life. She loved the creativity of planning a garden, the satisfaction of growth. She could not garden in her backyard in Limbo because she lacked the strength in her fingers, had no tools, and had no seeds, but each day she could examine the state of health and growth of the plants already there.

Besides the sagebrush, she had grasses, sedges, and rushes: short, vigorous tufts of reddish brown, long elegant fronds of grayish green, stiff spikes of dark jade topped with ragged brown heads. She had noticed that some stems were round and some were triangular, some stood straight as soldiers and some drooped gracefully, nodding in the breeze.

She had discovered micro-habitats in her backyard.

Certain plants grew in the shade of the building where the heavy morning dew lingered, others preferred a hot, dry location; some plants liked the company of other plants, and some were solitary.

She also had wildflowers. Cups of small grey leaves with soft white flower heads adorned the dirt between the sagebrush bushes. A low-growing spiky shrub with delicate orange blossoms, bloomed beside her back step. Her favorite was the secret lily, the one tiny flower that shyly hid amongst the stiff bristles of prairie grass. If she had possessed a field guide in English, she could have identified it as a sego lily.

She cherished the lily as if it was her best friend, and checked on its wellbeing every morning. If tea had been part of her afterlife, she would have sipped a morning cup with the lily. As it was, she started each day by chatting with the lily, before making her rounds to her other favored plants, accompanied by the herd of cats that lived in and around her house.

The chat was in Chinese, which neither the cats nor the lily understood. Her voice was like a wren's, a continuous, melodic burble. The cats did understand that her message was friendly.

The silent child in the brush could not understand what she was saying either, but, after listening for a few minutes, he, too, decided that The Chinese Lady must be a friendly person.

The hound dog stepped forward and woofed.

CHAPTER FIFTEEN:

The Long Way Home

After the poker game broke up, there was nothing to do but go home, and Alyse didn't want to do that. Without the focus of the game, there wasn't much to keep the group together. She didn't want to hang out in front of the saloon listening to Warren being sardonic and Jack being cynical. Trey had wandered off to check on Scotty, who was only prevented from being suicidal because he was already dead. She could feel herself sagging into the black hole of boredom and depression. If she was going to be bored and depressed, she preferred to do it alone.

As she drifted toward her shack, she thought about just drifting out of town, down the dirt road, on and on, as Jack had done so many times and could do again. She could see why that prospect would excite his interest: the hope that there might be *something* in the next outpost, something to care about.

Her shack did not feel like home. She had never

minded going home when she was alive. Her mind filled with going-home memories: her brisk saunter across the grass to the school parking lot, waving to friends, jingling her car keys, or being dropped at the curb by a friend after a party or after a track meet. Home had been her launch pad—safe, secure—and she had been so sure that she would soon blast off like a rocket, into adult life, into a meaningful orbit.

Now going home meant defeat. She didn't want to stare at the unforgiving brown walls or sit and gaze out over the relentless expanse of grey-green sage and infinite sky. She didn't want to sit around, alone and lonely, knowing she'd failed and with nothing to do.

She felt hollow and sick. How could she feel sick when she had no stomach? She hunched over, wrapping her arms around her midrift. Her arms sank into her body, a disgusting reminder of her ghostliness. Suddenly she wanted her mother. Right there in the middle of the dusty street, she wanted her mother.

She didn't want anyone to see her cry.

Alyse lifted her arms, threw her hair back over her shoulders, and took to the air.

She swooped straight up, seeking height, with her eyes on the smooth unblemished blue of the robin's egg sky. The village dropped beneath her until it was nothing but a ragged streak of brown, like a scab on a wound. She looked down, twirled in place, and gathered herself into a little ball. She wondered what would happen if she just kept going up, up, up into the sky.

The wind carried her toward the mountains, out

over the sea of sage and grass. Alyse spread her arms out like wings and lay on the air. She floated over the wandering line of green that marked the river. She drifted high enough to see the translucent violet-blue of the distant mountains stretching in a panorama from one end of the horizon to the other. She felt the wind blowing through her, like the river water. Her body undulated.

She realized that, from the air, the land was almost as colorful as the rocks in the river. More subtly colored, but just as varied. The prairie was not just yellow, but greenish silver, tan, dun, gold, and orange in shimmering layers. The shadows were not just purple, but reflected green with a turquoise aura. The sky shaded to lilac over the mountains. The colors made her think of her sister, Andee.

She began to talk to her sister in her mind, describing the landscape and the colors. Andee would be grabbing her paints if she could see the view. She would make something beautiful out of Limbo. Alyse wished that Andee were there, too, flying with her.

She imagined herself describing the feeling of flying: the air beneath her outstretched arms, cool and bouncy, the way she could extend her limbs outward, clear to her fingers and toes, as no earthbound person could ever do.

She saw a hawk. It rode the air, circling lazily, relaxed, adjusting to the wind with just a tip of its wings.

She tried it, circling, tipping her fingers a bit to stay level. She wished her sister was there to fly with her, but it was not a sad wish. She realized that her mood had changed. The bright air had blown away her depression.

Then she thought, why stay level? She rolled, making the ground and the air reverse and reverse again until she was dizzy.

She experimented with dance and tumbling runs. She went from a somersault to an arabesque to a twirl. She did a series of long swan dive swoops that shot exhilarating blasts of adrenalin through her nervous system. Flying was like being an Olympic gymnast or a ballet dancer, only better. She realized that she felt happy, except that she had no one to be happy with her.

She liked the way her long hair flew out behind her. Sexy, she thought. Except for the bald spot on the left side, the side with the stitches.

Then she thought that it was too bad no guy would ever appreciate her long hair, never see her as sexy, flying in the sky. And through that door, sad thoughts entered her mind, and some of the fun leaked out.

She circled down slowly, a new heaviness entering her heart.

As the village grew larger, and buildings gained distinction, she realized that she was over the far end of town, near the church and The Chinese Lady's house. She aimed for the steeple.

Since she didn't want to go home, she landed on the church roof. Maybe she could hang on to some last wisp of her good mood if she saw the sunset from a different spot. She settled with her back against the steeple.

She became aware that The Chinese Lady was in her back yard. Since she had not previously paid much attention to The Chinese Lady, she moved slightly for better observation and settled down to do some spying. Then she realized that there was a small figure with The Chinese Lady, a boy, a ragged child. They were sitting together on The Chinese Lady's back step. The hound dog lay curled at their feet.

Alyse stared with fascination. In her time in Limbo there had been no children. She had been the youngest. She had assumed that had something to do with a capacity for sin. Now she was looking down at a boy of no more than ten at the most. He was small compared to The Chinese Lady, who was pretty short herself.

And what were they doing? The Chinese Lady had a stick. She was drawing in the dirt. Alyse could not make out the picture. She watched the woman and the child study the picture. The Chinese Lady pointed and repeated a sound. The boy mimicked her words.

She's teaching him Chinese, Alyse thought in surprise. Then, why not? Why assume The Chinese Lady had to learn English?

Alyse wanted to go down and learn Chinese too, but there was an intimacy between the two figures that kept her away. So, she watched.

Then she saw The Chinese Lady wrap her arms around the child. She absorbed the child inside her chest. Alyse could see his curved back through the encompassing shape of the Chinese lady, like a baby in a womb.

Alyse began to cry silently. She crept around to the

far side of the steeple, so as not to bother The Chinese Lady and the child, and wept. She wept because she was lonely, because she wanted to be able to tell her sister about the colors in the landscape, tell her parents about her friend, Trey, or tell someone alive about flying.

After a while she sat up and surveyed the town. A few people were out and about. She could see Jack on the roof of the saloon, watching a glorious orange sunset deepen into rose. She wondered about the villagers she could not see. Trey was probably with Scotty, trying to cheer him up.

The poor Naked Man was alone somewhere. Darla and Lily, what did they do when they were alone?

She had nowhere else to go but home.

CHAPTER SIXTEEN:
Almost Heaven

Alyse had been waiting the next morning for Trey, eager to tell him about flying and about The Chinese Lady and the little boy, but instead the question popped out of her mouth, "How come kids don't automatically go to Heaven?" She considered Trey a resource on all matters religious, although she often did not accept his ideas.

"There's a little boy here." She told Trey about the child she had seen with The Chinese Lady. She did not mention how The Chinese Lady had enfolded the child into herself. "What could he have done that would keep him out of Heaven? He's just a little boy."

"I don't know," said Trey. "We all have original sin."

"I don't believe that. I know we aren't all perfect but . . . what kind of god would punish a kid?"

"I don't know," said Trey. "Maybe the kid came here because it isn't so bad. I told you, I'm kind of glad I died."

Alyse did not remember Trey saying that.

"This ain't Hell," Trey added.

"I know," Alyse argued, "but The Preacher thinks we're here because we are all sinners, so that's like a punishment—not as bad as Hell, but punishment regardless."

"Well, maybe he's right. That's what he believes." Trey wasn't going to argue about religion with anyone. He mulled over Alyse's comments. Of course, everyone who arrived in Limbo spent time thinking about their new situation. Everyone spent time trying to fit their experience of the afterlife into the religious convictions they had brought with them. For some, those religious convictions were discarded like winter clothes on a tropical cruise. Others were able to make some kind of match between expectations and experience. Trey had expected eternal happiness, kind of like a continuous supply of Zoloft, but was willing to settle for being free of pain.

"Being here isn't all that different from being alive," Trey observed. "Everyone's got to die, and this ain't all that bad for an afterlife."

Alyse experienced a disconcerting shift in perspective, an internal earthquake. Trey meant it when he said he didn't mind being dead. He was not a happy person, but, for the first time, she realized that he was a reasonably contented one.

"So you're saying that this is not really punishment. I mean it sucks being dead, or it sucks for me, but evidently that's how God made things. Everyone dies, so here I am, and it isn't necessarily all that bad?"

Trey gazed off into the distance. "I don't know. I don't really want to tell anyone what to believe."

They settled into one of their long mutual silences. Alyse's thoughts made tentative excursions into unfamiliar territory. "So we should just make the best of it? Is that what you are saying?"

She could imagine her mother saying that. "Stop fussing. Make the best of a bad situation."

Or her dad saying, "What? An afterlife with no books?"

Alyse grinned. Then she frowned, thinking that she would never see her mom or dad again. They'd be somewhere else in Limbo. Why was that the rule? Why weren't they allowed to see their loved ones again?

"I guess I could get to know some more people here," Trey commented. His mind had been moving along a different track. "I don't have much to say to Darla most of the time. To tell the truth, she scares me. But I like that black guy."

"I don't like Darla either." Alyse tried to pull her thoughts closer to Trey's. The truth was she didn't like very many of the villagers. "But I'd like to get to know Emmanuel." It was part of Alyse's social training that she could never refer to anyone by color. "I think I'd also like to get to know The Chinese Lady. And the kid."

And, she thought, we should have helped The Naked Man somehow.

"You know what I'd like to do?" Trey asked wistfully.

"What?"

"I'd like to have a party. I'd like to have a party with dancing." He nodded. "That's what I would like to do."

CHAPTER SEVENTEEN:
The Pissing Contest

It turned out that, before they could have a party, there had to be a fight.

Trey and Alyse asked Darla if she wanted to help organize the party and asked The Preacher if he wanted to talk to the choir about singing. Inevitably, that led to a discussion between The Preacher and Darla about the party.

They met in front of Darla's house on the main street. Darla's place looked like it had once been a store; there was a boardwalk out front, and a hitching rail for horses. Darla used the boardwalk as a front porch and platform for her unelected position as Mayoress.

Darla greeted The Preacher graciously, invited him up onto her porch, and proceeded to tell him the plans for the community event.

"We'll need the church because it's the nearest thing to a community center. The church is too small for dancing, so the party will be outside. We can't bring treats or drinks, but we can pick flowers or bring willow wands . . . ”

"If we are going to be outside, I can preach from the steps." The Preacher had a look in his eye, spoiling for a fight. Darla had a look in her eye, too. In fact, both had come to the conversation with that same look in their eyes. Darla and The Preacher had very little to say to each other under ordinary circumstances. He disliked her height, her narrow elegance, and her cool presumption of authority. She thought The Preacher was trailer trash.

"I don't know that preaching is appropriate for the party, do you?" Darla asked in that fake questioning way that bossy people use to issue decrees. "I don't think that it fits with the theme."

"There's a long tradition of preaching at community get-togethers," The Preacher asserted. "Traditional small town events featured preaching before the festivities. In this town, where we await God . . . ”

Darla cut him off, "Just because we appear to be in an Old West ghost town does not mean we are pioneers."

"But we are pioneers! We are the vanguard, the dead approaching God! We are part way between Earth and Heaven!" The Preacher bounced upwards for emphasis, his voice excitedly falling into the singsong of a sermon.

Darla waited for his head to return to eye level. She kept a firm grip on her composure and spoke with patience. "Preacher, this is a party, not a revival. A social get-together so people can have fun and become better acquainted. If you wish to have a revival, you can do so at some other time."

The Preacher sneered through gritted teeth. "You need to remember that Trey and Alyse came to me about using the choir—"

"The choir does not belong to you," Darla interrupted. "You do not own them. They are not your slaves."

That was a touchy remark since one of the choir members was African, and The Preacher was a Southerner, born and bred, and raised on the belief that no outsider understood the South. "Are you trying to make this a racial thing? This is supposed to be a community get-together in God's Limbo!"

Darla inhaled deeply before speaking with icy calm. "I am not turning this into a racial anything. I am simply pointing out that the choir does not belong to you and does not work for you. You brought race into it yourself."

"No, I didn't!" The Preacher was getting shrill now as he lost ground. "You said I was treating Emmanuel as if he were a slave, and he is not even American!"

"Oh." Darla crossed her arms and lifted her chin. "So you have a different attitude toward Africans than toward African Americans?"

By now a small crowd of villagers had gathered, hoping that the fight would move beyond mere verbal pot shots.

"Stop making it a race thing. Everyone here is gray!" Exasperated, The Preacher broke into a shout.

Darla smirked, "Yes we are all gray, but some of us

are more transparent than others."

Fueled by anger, both Darla and The Preacher had risen to about ten feet above street level. On-lookers had to crane their necks to watch. Both adversaries were glaring, and The Preacher had begun to windmill his arms.

"What are you insinuating?" The Preacher demanded. "Don't you know that the word 'sin' is in the word 'insinuation'?"

"This is not the time for clever word play," Darla twisted her lips dismissively on the word 'clever'. "I am going to ask the members of the choir if they, singly or as a group, would like to perform secular," she hit that word hard, "secular music for our event."

The Preacher shoved his face into hers and snapped, "And I will ask if they would like to uplift us with—"

A stray breeze caught The Preacher's hospital gown and blew it open, revealing his rounded flanks and fat thighs. He flapped his arms, smacking the windblown cloth back in place. Hit by the breeze, he lost control and surged forward almost into an embrace with Darla. She quickly wafted backwards to get out of the way, her own nightgown swirling and flapping.

Warren, watching the show, was reminded of dance: swirling hospital gowns, evocative arm movements, lots of bare leg visible. He decided to applaud.

The others watching laughed and applauded, too. Their laughter was audible, but their clapping was not.

Jack yelled, "Hurray! Great show guys!"

Darla, deeply embarrassed but determined to maintain her dignity, descended to street level with the appearance of calm.

She issued a general announcement to the watchers, "I will talk to the choir about our party." She swept grandly through the wall of her house and disappeared.

The Preacher descended without grace, glaring at Jack. "You weren't being very helpful. All you do is stand around and sneer at everyone."

Warren, who was much better at standing around and sneering than Jack, observed quietly that The Preacher's gown was now up around his armpits.

CHAPTER EIGHTEEN:
The Preacher Strikes Back

The Preacher was rehearsing. He worked hard on his sermons. Throughout the week he was alert for little incidents, comments, events that could connect to a Biblical text and serve as a basis for a lesson on living. He believed that the Bible was a road map. He believed that each day was an opportunity for a human being to do better in living as God expected. Darla had given him such an opportunity.

His text for the upcoming Sunday was ". . . men will give an account on the Day of Judgment for every careless word they have spoken. For by your words you will be acquitted, and by your words you will be condemned."

Men and women, he thought. It was too bad Darla never attended the service, but others would be there and they would know who he was talking about.

He savored the quote. He ran the words through his mouth, letting them roll around like chocolate, sweet and satisfying. Yep, he had the hook for a really satisfying sermon.

One of his many regrets about finding himself in Limbo was the absence of a Bible; he could not remember very many references word for word. He remembered stories and could paraphrase passages, but he couldn't recall the exact wording of significant texts. He didn't understand why God had separated him from the Bible, unless it was punishment for failing to have memorized more of it, but he believed, he had to believe, that someday he would see the words again. Someday he would read the sacred words again.

So he practiced his sermons based on what he could recall. He practiced by standing in the air about four feet off the ground, with good posture, shoulders back, eyes aimed where the parishioners would be. He thought his gray hospital gown made him look like an angel. He gestured frequently, since large arm movements made the garment fan out like wings. It didn't matter if the gown opened in the back, since he positioned himself only a few inches out from the wall.

"What do these words mean?" he asked his imaginary audience. He paused dramatically. Pausing was a good rhetorical device. It was important not to speak too quickly.

"It means that we need to be careful what we say about each other because our words are a reflection of us. If we see evil in someone else, it may be because the evil is familiar and recognizable because it is an evil we have ourselves. It's called projection. Psychiatrists use that word."

He was aware that his congregation included skeptics who attended for the music, so he tried to include secular backing for his religious lessons when he could.

"God is watching us," he said. "He is watching your behavior and my behavior and the behavior of people everywhere. He sees how each person talks about and to other people. God does not listen to gossip. God does not listen to the bad things you say about other people and then thinks you're telling the truth. God listens to the bad things you say about others and then thinks badly of you."

He continued, "If you had a calendar, then every day that you say something bad about another person is another day to add to living here in Limbo. We are here in a waiting room, waiting for our turn to shine. We are trying to show God that we are good enough for Heaven. We need to show that we are working on our own behavior, not judging others. Let's pray on the words of God."

He repeated his quote from Matthew with relish, thinking of Darla. Ha! It was a good sermon. He needed to practice it a few more times, get it to roll off the tongue with planned pauses. Keep it to the point, no straying. He was proud of it.

CHAPTER NINETEEN:
Emmanuel

Emmanuel began his vocal exercises precisely when the sun completed its emergence from behind the cottonwood tree in back of his shack. He had been sitting on the back steps waiting for this moment, just sitting for . . . he wasn't sure how long. Long enough to hear three distinct bird songs and the distant yodel of a coyote. But now the sun was officially up, based on his definition of sunrise, so he arose and let out a matching yodeling wail of his own.

Just a weak yodel, a thin thread of sound that spun into the air like a spider web. He was always cautious with his first vocalization of the day; he allowed his throat and his vocal cords a bit of warning before cutting loose. He thought of his voice as an entity separate from himself. His first vocalization of the day was a gentle shake on his voice's shoulder. Wake up, sleepyhead.

Once sleepyhead was awake, Emmanuel gradually

built in volume. He ran the scales. He hit individual notes independently, holding each without a wobble. He listened to himself carefully, and measured out doses of sound in smoothly rounded units, like bubbles.

In life he had not been conscientious about vocal exercises, but in Limbo what else was there to do? God had, for whatever reason, given him this time, this period between life and Heaven, and the only purpose he could see was to prepare himself for judgment. He was not at all certain what he should be doing in preparation. Limbo was a surprise, not part of his religious upbringing. He had expected some kind of afterlife, but he had largely abandoned the epic dramas of his Pentecostal childhood, and the sweet, kindly sermons of his Methodist adulthood had been more focused on how to live one's life than what to expect afterwards.

He had traveled so far in his life: from Ghana to America, from the home of an African shopkeeper to the suburbs of Boston, from his father's intense striving to his own success as a doctor, from belief in the great drama of God's will to a quiet skepticism, and then, at last, to a strange ghost town in the desert.

He thought God must have dropped him into a desert for some reason; the sere, silvery landscape was so different from the overwhelming greenery of his childhood home. He was floundering in the stark landscape, unable to settle or focus his thoughts. He tried to impose order on his day with a routine, in hopes that, by organizing the exterior of his existence, he might find something solid in the interior.

Since singing was his gift, he sang each day until he could sing no more. Then he waited for the next day so he could sing again.

He knew his exercises were annoying to Jack the Traveler, who did not want to wake up with the sun. Jack wanted to sleep until the damned old sun was straight up or headed toward the other horizon. He sometimes expressed his displeasure by shouting obscenities out his window. He routinely referred to Emmanuel as "that rooster" or "that cock." Or obscene variations on the word "cock".

Emmanuel's exercises achieved an extra level of verve and volume at the thought of waking Jack up. Perhaps that was his Pentecostal childhood asserting itself; he had been raised to believe that it was his duty to convert others to the true religion. Since he no longer believed in the four square gospel himself, he had no desire to convert others in that direction, but he could not break himself of the habit of trying to influence aspects of other people's behavior. Maybe that was why he became a doctor: so he could spend his life lecturing people on their lifestyle choices.

There was no sound from next door. Jack was either still asleep, or had decided not to shout.

Exercises done, Emmanuel moved on to singing. The first step was to find a good private location because, while he rather enjoyed bothering Jack with exercises, the process of practicing the delivery of a song was something he wanted to do without an audience. Besides, looking for a good singing spot took up more of the day, and Emmanuel needed time fillers.

So he set out on a jaunt into the countryside. Usually he headed south since his back step faced that way, but this morning he went through his house, out through the front wall, and into the street. He had decided to go north in search of a good spot.

He emerged into the street at about the same time as Darla. She immediately flagged him down with a wave of her arm and a "hello".

"Good morning, Darla." Out of good manners Emmanuel hid his surprise at her greeting. He had excellent manners, magnified by his accented English, which gave even his casual comments a formal sound.

"Good morning," Darla chirped. "I was going to look you up this afternoon, but here you are! This is certainly serendipitous!"

Emmanuel didn't know if he believed in serendipity. His parents had no doubt that everything that happened was intentional, the planned will of God. While he was not sure God was micro-managing the details of human existence, Emmanuel did have a sense of the importance of minor events. He believed that the butterfly flapping its wings in China could set off a ripple of action and reaction around the world. He had chosen to go north that morning rather than south, and that little decision had led to bumping into Darla who he did not normally chat with much, and Darla was clearly up to something. Thus his decision to go north could have unexpected consequences and might be part of a larger plan. Emmanuel smiled and raised his eyebrows while waiting to see what she wanted.

"I suppose you have heard of the proposed party?"

Darla asked. "Trey and Alyse asked me to organize it. The idea is to have a fun community event for all of us."

"Oh yes, The Preacher mentioned that." Poor little Alyse who had died young, and Trey, a man so quiet that his personality was even less visible than his ghost body. They wanted a party. It seemed an odd desire, but harmless.

"We, that's Trey, Alyse and I, are hoping you will lend your wonderful singing voice to some music for the party, something cheerful. Maybe songs people can clap to or even dance to."

For a brief moment, Emmanuel wondered if she thought he could rap or sing hip hop or whatever kind of music white Americans associated with black people. He was too used to white Americans trying to fit him into their stereotypes of black Americans to be offended. He had spent his adult life gently reminding people that, as an immigrant from Ghana, America's neurosis about race had nothing to do with him. It never occurred to him that his assertion that American race relations were irrelevant to his life was incongruent with the constant need he had to keep pointing out the irrelevance.

"I'm not sure I know any appropriate songs," Emmanuel responded politely, "though I would very much like to be part of the effort to have a party."

"I'm sure we can figure something out." Darla was one of those people who pressured others by smiling hard at them until they capitulated to her demands. Emmanuel was willing to be agreeable with her, but was unsure of what he was actually agreeing to.

"I know some religious songs," he said, "but I'm not sure they are appropriate for a party."

"I think you are right," Darla responded, delighted to find Emmanuel on her side against The Preacher. "This will not be a religious occasion. Do you know any folk songs?"

Folk songs? Emmanuel's mind was blank on the topic of American folk songs. He had sung in churches all his life, the raucous jubilant Pentecostal church of his childhood and the more sedate mainline church of his professional life in Boston. He could belt out a pretty good "Messiah" at Christmas time. For The Preacher and the little neighborhood church, he sang the more obvious hymns like "Amazing Grace."

For himself, off on his own, he sang show tunes and love ballads.

He said, "I hate to disappoint you, Darla, but I don't think I know the kind of songs you need. If you can come up with a list of songs, and some of the other choir members can teach the songs to me, I will be glad to sing for you. I just don't know the right songs for you."

He started backing away from her fierce, demanding smile, as her face stiffened into a mask of politesse.

"You let me know, won't you?" Emmanuel said, and he gave a polite nod in farewell. He left Darla smiling hard at his retreating back.

He escaped out over the roofs on the north side of the street and kept going out over the prairie.

CHAPTER TWENTY:
Party Poopers

Jack picked up his cards. They were playing five-card draw for a change. He fiddled his cards, deliberately moving them around more than necessary, to make his hand look weak. "So," he said, tilting his head to one side, "Who do you think won yesterday's pissing contest?"

"You mean our two alphas?" Warren asked.

"Alphas? I'll buy Darla as an alpha male, but not The Preacher."

"The Preacher's a wimp. What does he know?" Lily glared at her hand.

"Why do alphas have to be males?" Alyse challenged. "Darla being alpha doesn't make her less of a woman. She's still female."

Jack's arched his eyebrows. "I just didn't want to call her a bitch in mixed company. I'll take two."

It was Alyse's deal. Her dealing style was earnest and careful. She handed Jack two cards face down. She wanted to argue that being a strong female didn't make Darla a bitch, but Darla was kind of bitchy. Something had made her that way.

"Three here," said Warren. "And I think Darla won that round with The Preacher. If we're going to place bets on a rematch, I'm going with her."

"Huh, three," said Lily. "Won't be no rematch. Preacher will stay out of her way now."

"Two for me." Alyse dealt cards to herself. They all studied their hands. Alyse found it hard to concentrate. She was thinking that the poker players weren't like what grownups were supposed to be. She had expected grownups to be, well, more adult: wiser, better behaved. The poker players acted like girls in the school cafeteria, saying catty things about whoever walked by. She had thought that they'd be . . . kinder than that. And they hadn't said a word about the party idea. Even Trey hadn't mentioned it.

"You gonna call for bets or what?" Lily asked.

Later on that evening Alyse searched out Trey and Scotty in their cabin at the north end of town. She found them perched on the roof of Trey's humble shack. The shack was just one small room with an enclosed back porch, so the roof did not give them much altitude. The front step was too small for two people to share, which left the roof as the only other option. Trey greeted Alyse with, "Hey there, come on up." Scotty moved over so she could sit between the two men.

After she settled herself, Scotty asked, "So what's up?" He waggled his eyebrows in a clumsy attempt to be jovial. Scotty was not used to being around young women.

"Well . . . " Alyse let the word drag out. "It doesn't seem like the party idea is catching on." She waited, hoping they would reassure her.

"No booze," Scotty explained. "Can't have a party with no booze 'cuz people gotta loosen up, get happy, you know? No one wants to just hang out."

Nevermind that just hanging out was exactly what they were doing, the three of them perched in a row on the peak of the roof. Scotty was still twitchy, but Alyse knew that Trey was reasonably content just hanging out. She was, too, she realized with surprise. She was sitting between a dead drunk and a dead Texan on the roof of a shack in a ghost town in the desert, and she was reasonably content. She wished she could tell her mother and laugh about it.

She could not afford to think about her family.

Think about having a party instead.

"I think we could have a party without booze. We just need to think of a theme for it." She inserted confidence into her voice and lifted her chin.

"That's cause you're just a kid," Scotty said. He made his comment without rancor. He simply meant that Alyse was still young enough to get enjoyment out of existence without being drunk, an ability he had lost many, many years previously.

"You're going to have a hard time firing up this bunch," he added, meaning the townsfolk.

He was right. She would have a hard time firing up the townsfolk. She was having a hard time firing up Trey, and it was his idea.

Alyse thought of a story from her life to tell. It bothered her a lot that everyone had stories except her. Scotty had stories of his military service, Trey had stories of West Texas, she had nothing but a life of nice, clean, upper middle-class comfort and security.

"I can fire people up," she said. "I made my high school change the prom night date. That wasn't easy."

The two men looked at her with identical quizzical expressions.

"Well, the prom is important! I mean it is the high point of high school! Didn't you guys go to the prom at your school?"

"I didn't go," said Trey. "I was working, I think. That was just before I got married."

"I went," Scotty grinned, showing the gaps in his teeth. "I went with this little gal named Sally, and I spent a bunch of money on her and got a home run for it. Ha!"

Alyse edged a bit away from Scotty and toward Trey. She sat up straight, the better to get their attention, determined to tell her story. "Well, the prom was important at my school. Everyone went to it. Even the juniors were allowed to go, for practice for when they were seniors."

She checked with sideways glances; both men were watching her face. "I was on the track team, and we were doing really well that year. I didn't get a state medal, but two of the other girls did, and we were a top-ranked team. Anyway, the most important track meet of the year was the same day that the prom was scheduled. And that meant I'd have to get home and shower and get dressed up after the meet," Alyse's voice stumbled, and she hurried on. "I knew I wouldn't be able to get ready in time and neither would anyone else on the track team, boys or girls. So I went in to ask that the date be changed."

She remembered the day vividly. On that day, she had demonstrated civil tenacity and assertiveness, just as her parents had taught her. She had knocked politely on the Vice-Principal's door, and had stood before his desk as a student seeking redress of grievances. She had made her pitch in well-practiced sentences, articulate and logical.

"I just explained to him that we were representing the school at state, and we should not be penalized for that by not being able to be our best at the dance too." A trace of defiance entered her voice. She could see herself in the office, in front of the Vice-Principal's desk, being responsible and assertive, but somehow the scene was playing out differently with Scotty and Trey as the audience. She remembered her skintight stretchy knit top and tight jeans, her body swaying as she spoke. Her fingers flipping her hair off her shoulder.

Had she really been flirting with the Vice-Principal?

Demanding a change in the prom date, while Trey was working and getting married for his.

She remembered the Vice-Principal, lounging at his desk, chair pushed back, a very handsome man who almost looked white with his closely clipped hair and caramel skin. He had been aware of her flirtatiousness.

He had been aware. And she had thought he was handsome because he almost looked white.

Had she really thought that way: handsome because he almost looked white?

Alyse realized that she had stopped talking. Trey and Scotty were waiting for the end of her story. She rushed into speech, "Anyway, I just asked him nicely if he could change the date, and he said 'OK' and moved the dance night one day over from Friday to Saturday so I—I mean, we—could go."

She tried to end the story with a flourish of triumph, but the story had not come out as she had intended. It was supposed to be a story about how she had been assertive, to show that she could fire people up and give a party for Trey. Instead it was a story of her being flirtatious with an adult and maybe racist. And selfish.

She couldn't even look at Trey.

His hand went into her thigh, a friendly ghost pat. "You sure were a smart kid."

Alyse sneaked a look at his face. Trey was serious. "I bet you could get about anything you set out to get," he said with admiration.

Alyse would have blushed if she had been able. Instead she said, "Well, I just think your party idea is a good one, and I'd like to see it happen."

"We'll figure it out," Trey assured her.

CHAPTER TWENTY-ONE:
Singing to the Cows

Emmanuel could hear cows in the distance. He could barely see them; the waist high thickets of sagebrush and greasewood blocked his view, but he could hear the gentle snuffling, the odd grunts and groans that made the herd sound like wooden ships settling into the waves.

He wondered what the cows were saying. Was it friendly chatter, like a bunch of women, walkers in a Boston park, elbow-to-elbow, striding along with lung capacity sufficient to sustain conversation? No . . . cows didn't stride. Even though he couldn't see them well, he knew how they moved. They strolled, lumbering along with heavy shoulder movements, their sturdy legs rammed into the dust by their great barrel-shaped bodies.

Emmanuel had walked for about a mile out into the prairie before coming to a stopping place. It was not a place much different than any other place on the long incline from the mountains to the river. He had stopped because of the cows. They formed a wall of sorts, gave him a reason to come to a halt, a decision that otherwise would have been arbitrary.

He didn't mind having cows as an audience. Cows had been part of his childhood. The rural and the urban tended to mix in Ghana, particularly in the suburbs where his father had kept shop. Cows, dogs, chickens, and children all hung out in the mud together on hot days. Sometimes he had been frightened by the dogs, but never the cows with their big brown eyes and soft noses.

Had he, in a way, returned home? To mix with cows and dogs on the edge of a community? He didn't think so, not really. He felt lost between the highly abstracted optimism of his wife's religion and the grand operatic drama of the religion of his childhood. Neither included this strange place.

Both included the notion that life was to be led purposefully, that there was a reason for getting out of bed in the morning, a reason to go places and do things. To his parents, human life was part of an all-encompassing narrative that went back thousands of years and would reach a magnificent climax some day in the future. To his wife, life was simply a matter of doing some good every now and then while not being completely given over to shopping.

He had lived his whole life with a sense that God was watching. Not participating. Just watching. Now he was sure. Now he got up in the morning certain that every day was a test of how he chose to spend his time.

It seemed his choices were limited. There were so many, many things he could not do or no longer needed to do. In fact, most of the choices that had once been available to him were gone. He had no career or need of one. He didn't need to eat, grocery shop, put gas in the car, or mow the lawn. He didn't need to get dressed, take a shower, or get a haircut. He didn't need to buy anything, there was nothing to read, nothing to watch on TV, nothing to fix, and no one he was obligated to interact with. He could wake up or not. He could go outside or not. He could chat with other villagers, although many were unfriendly or sad or angry, like people stranded in a bus station in a snowstorm.

Or he could ignore the other villagers.

He could go for a walk, or not.

He could sing.

And, while singing, he could try to figure it out. Why had he been given an afterlife?

He inhaled deeply, wondering briefly how that was possible without lungs. His ghostly anatomy interested him from a scientific point of view, and sometimes he examined himself, looking for something more than a faintly pearly grayness indicating an old bathrobe, PJs, and slippers, but there was nothing. Nothing to breathe with, but he did breathe. He inhaled again because it felt good.

He sang. He let one note sit on the air, let it extend out, hovering over the sagebrush like a hummingbird. He was aware of the vast blue sky and ocean of silvery green vegetation. Somewhere a bird answered him with a ripple of song. He changed to a higher note, and then a lower one.

Then Emmanuel went deep into his chest and pulled out the lines of a show tune, "Old Man River." He made the words rumble like a barrel rolling down a gangplank. When he got to the lines about sweating and working, he stopped. Those lines did not suit his mood or his experience. He no longer needed to tote bales, figuratively speaking.

He wanted a happier song. He set the word "I" out on the air, sustained it, made it lift and fall wavelike before diving into the rest of the line. Dolly Parton, that's me, he grinned to himself. Women always sang that song, but men can love, too.

Had he loved his wife? He had certainly been comfortable with her ways. They had been compatible, which was amazing really, given their differing backgrounds. He had done most of the adapting. At some level he had used her. She had been his island in America, and he had settled on that island like a limpet on a rock. He had grown to see himself through her eyes as quaint and funny, one of those musical Africans who were so poor, but plucky and full of initiative. She had never wanted to visit Ghana.

She had died first. He often wondered where she was in Limbo and how she spent each day. She had been a pediatrician, had really loved children. It would be hard for her to be in a place with so few kids, just as it had been hard for her to realize that she would never be a mother.

He felt a stirring in his heart for her, wherever she was. So devoted to children. He hoped her end of Limbo had kids. "I will always . . . miss you," he sang, ending the song almost in a whisper. His happy song had somehow turned sad.

Enough of that, he told himself. He straightened up, took in another chest full of air and thought. A song for this beautiful day. Because the day was lovely: soft, gentle, a creation in pastels and iridescence. He lifted his arms and felt the air moving through his limbs, his chest, and his face. This must be what it is like to be a sheet on a clothesline, he thought. One of the cows mooed, a contented sound.

He pulled in air and let it out sensuously, making himself part of the gentle breeze. Words of a song came to him: "My life flows on in endless song above earth's lamentations."

He began to sing. It was hard to hit a high note on "lam" without getting a bit screamy. He started over, singing more gently, emphasizing "on". He moved the 'men' to the high note. That worked.

He started through the song again, carefully fitting the syllables to the melody, experimenting with emphasis. Halfway through, he realized that he did not quite remember the words. No matter, he just made some up. When he had worked the song to his satisfaction, he faced downhill, inhaled deeply, and sang to the sagebrush and the sky and the cows and the bright clean air.

CHAPTER TWENTY-TWO:
The Life Raft

Alyse and Trey went to church together, which felt odd to Alyse. She had not gone to church with her own family. To be out in public, attending church with an adult male, made her question the relationship. What was she to Trey: friend, neighbor? She kept a careful space between them.

They situated themselves in the back just inside the door, where Trey, a very large man, was most comfortable. The church interior was cramped and crowded, the brown walls obscured by the gray ghosts floating in the air or leaning against the wall: a haunted house, festooned with gray shapes. We look like spider webs, Alyse thought.

She looked around to see who was attending. Up front, Lily was on her knees as if in supplication, though, judging by her expression, she was not in a prayerful frame of mind. The others Alyse knew by name but not much else: seven women and a couple of men, mostly old, mostly in hospital gowns, and one lady had her hair in curlers. Alyse felt a stab of pity while suppressing a giggle; what a fate to spend eternity in curlers! They were, indeed, a dreary bunch of people. If it wasn't for the singing and Trey, she would not have come to church.

The choir hung along one wall: three ladies and two gentleman. The singer with the best voice was a large African named Emmanuel, who spoke thick, heavily-accented English. The other male singer was a skinny white man whose clear tenor was nearly inaudible behind the robust booming voice of the African. The three women were thin-voiced sopranos who could just about carry a tune, if they had a bucket handy.

Listen to me, Alyse thought. I'm thinking such snarky things. The three ladies are doing us all a favor by singing.

Alyse sucked in her breath and squared her shoulders, as if she could rearrange her thoughts by straightening out her body. She liked the singing. She didn't have anything better to do that morning. The other services she'd attended had not been a waste of time. Even though there was something icky about The Preacher, even though he thought he was God's gift to ghosts, even though his sermons were only thought provoking by accident, still she could find *something* worthwhile in the next hour, if she tried.

Lousy start. Try again. She was just mad because no one was responding to her party idea with any enthusiasm, except The Preacher, which was like having your idea endorsed by the biggest loser in town. Stop it, Alyse! The Preacher is just a guy doing his best.

Alyse made herself listen. The Preacher clearly had his sermon rehearsed to the last gesture and facial expression. He provided pauses in his word flow for those members of the audience who needed to shout "Amen" or break into spontaneous prayer.

His sermon was on the topic of gossip, how the mean things people said reflected on the person who said them, rather than the target of the gossip. An appropriate sermon; Alyse shifted position uncomfortably. Her mean thoughts reflected on her. He's just doing his best, Alyse told herself again. And he was trying to do good for all of them. She should be more willing to give him credit for that.

She wished she could be more like Trey, who always saw people as better than they really were.

The Preacher finished with a flourish. He seemed very pleased with himself. About half the attendees murmured "Amen" or "Yes, Lord", some of them swaying, eyes closed.

Alyse could not stop herself from reacting with distaste; such displays seemed like sucking up. She didn't think anyone would get to Heaven by currying favor. She just wanted the singing to start. Then she noticed Lily, still on her knees, looking fragile, broken, like an unwanted doll sprawled on the floor. Her thin shoulders were shaking as if she was crying. Alyse felt a shockwave of compassion. She wanted to say something to Lily, maybe ask if she was OK, but there was no way to reach her without disturbing the service. Alyse glanced at Trey and touched his arm to get his attention. He was frowning at Lily too. Trey shrugged and muttered, "I don't know."

The choir burst into song, Emmanuel's voice rumbling beneath the ringing voices of the sopranos. They sang "Farther Along," a hymn which posits that humans, after death, will be able to understand life. Alyse sang, too, quietly. While she sang, she thought about the lyrics. She was sure that the song was mistaken; after all, they were dead, but still full of questions. They had experienced no great understanding of life's mysteries. Would there be any answers farther along, after some other transition? She didn't think so. Maybe they were supposed to be figuring it out right here, right now.

Or, maybe they were supposed to have figured it out already, while they were still alive. Now they were on overtime, given another chance at the same puzzle.

She looked around the church, studying the faces. Emmanuel, given over to music. The choir ladies were swaying fervently, eyes on the ceiling. Trey's lips were moving, but soundlessly. He had no singing voice, but loved music. Lily, who had always seemed as tough as a barbed wire, was sitting with her shoulders hunched clear up to her ears as if her body could barely contain her feelings.

What were they thinking? She was willing to bet that Lily was struggling with questions, and did not seem to be finding answers. Were the others wondering, or did they think they already knew the answers?

I don't even know what questions to ask, Alyse thought. She suddenly felt a kind of kinship with everyone in the room, even the fervent church ladies. They were all lost at sea, struggling to hang onto a life raft. It didn't matter if they grabbed on at different places. She threw her voice into the song, joining in with the others for the last verse and the chorus.

After the singing, in a babble of talk, the church meeting was over. Alyse and Trey moved slowly toward the exit. The Preacher liked to stand on the steps to say goodbye, surrounded by his church ladies, and Trey liked to stop to say thank you for the service. Lily eeled her way through the crowd and out the door. Alyse watched Lily fly up the street toward the saloon, making her getaway.

Such a sad state of affairs, Lily running away like The Naked Man, alone. Alyse slipped her hand into Trey's.

CHAPTER TWENTY-THREE:
Warren and The Naked Man

Warren headed out into the prairie. He floated above the dry grass and sagebrush until he was well away up the long slope toward the mountains. When the village was almost gone, almost out of sight, he stopped to take a closer look around. He settled down into the sagebrush and began a careful inspection, looking for life forms. Or afterlife forms.

If he had been at home, still alive, he probably would have been reading. Reading or grading essays or planning a lecture, though he had lectured enough that he no longer needed to plan much. Maybe skirmishing in some staff war. He would have been on the watch for attractive young females . . . but nothing would have interfered with his reading.

Warren liked to read. It didn't matter much what the topic was: history, light science, anthropology, art history, biography. He'd been an omnivore of reading material.

Now he was starving. It was that starvation that had driven him out of the house and out to the prairie after Dean. He had decided to study nature.

While living, he had been an urbanite. He had enjoyed café culture, people-watching, the ebb and flow of human affairs. There weren't many people to watch in Limbo. He knew everyone. It had taken him very little time to sort out the dynamics of the community: the axis of Darla and The Preacher, the handful of committed churchgoers, the resolute church avoiders, the poker players, and the loners. Like most villagers, he had few interactions with **The Chinese Lady** since she didn't speak English. He was interested in Emmanuel, had seen him as a potential friend, but somehow that interest had not been reciprocated. There were no attractive women.

There were people he could hang out with, people he could tolerate, and a few he avoided, but no one he liked very much, except Alyse, who was a nice kid, and pretty, though too young.

He was bored. The novelty had worn off. Like everyone else, Limbo had come to him as a shock. In his case, the very possibility of life after death had been a shock. Warren had been an atheist. So . . . given that there was life after death at all, a God of some sort must exist. Warren wanted to know more about that God, but he didn't know where to get any more information. There was no point in asking the others; they were either as confused as he was or had latched onto certainties that seemed to him to be banal self-deceptions.

How could anyone, even living a life after death, know anything about God? He knew nothing. That was his starting point. And he didn't know how to move on from that point. So he woke up each day with time on his hands, and nothing to do except let Dean out for his daily ramble while rambling about town himself. He knew he had to find a focus or he would become depressed, and it seemed sacrilegious to spend eternity being sad out of boredom.

After all, life after death was an opportunity, wasn't it? An opportunity to understand things he had not understood before.

So he had decided to make a study of the ecology of Limbo. He was familiar with basic concepts from biology and ecology, knew about nutrient cycles, predator/prey cycles, water cycles, the great rhythms of the earth. He knew enough to know that Limbo operated on different rules.

The weather, for example, was nearly the same every day: mild, sunny in the afternoons, and dewy in the mornings, with occasional light rain. There was no snow on the distant mountains, yet a river flowed by, a wide flat river, about knee deep in most places, with a good fast flow. Where did the water come from?

Given the weather, the landscape should have been much drier. And the animal life, from an ecological point of view, made no sense. He had been in Limbo long enough to notice that the cows did not give birth, and the calves did not grow up. Nor did the cats procreate and multiply.

The local birdlife included macaws and parrots. Other than the coyotes heard in the distance and the occasional hawk, Dean and the cats seemed to be the only predators. They subsisted on mice and rabbits. Or did they? He had never seen any dead animals. He had never seen a cat catch a mouse, or Dean kill a rabbit.

There were no seasons. The sun always rose in the same spot and dropped behind the mountains in the same place. There was no Big Dipper—he'd checked.

From a scientific point of view, Limbo made no sense. There had to be some non-scientific sense to it. There had to be underlying patterns and cycles, beyond the obvious one of a daily passing of the sun overhead.

He had set out that day to look for data with the hope that patterns would emerge. He had decided to start at ground level with an examination of the dirt itself, under and between the ubiquitous sagebrush bushes. Warren sank down into the sagebrush and flew slowly. Wending his way between bushes and flying low to the ground, he felt like a fish in water, sliding through water weeds. Or, maybe a submarine. He examined the ground.

He found tracks of a mouse. The footprints rambled all over the place. The mouse had been very busy. Gathering food, he supposed. What had the mouse been eating? Maybe grass seeds, there were plenty of those about.

Or maybe the mouse ate insects. Now that he was right down in the sagebrush, really looking, he could see bugs. He meandered around, peering at the twisted arms of the brush. He saw some brown beetles. Gray beetles. Ants: red ones and black ones. So, four species of bug. And a lizard!

Warren felt a leap of joy at the sight of a small, grayish brown lizard. Something to eat the bugs! He watched the lizard. It did nothing at all. Beetles crawled in the sand within inches of its nose, and it remained still.

Well, maybe the lizard was not hungry. Warren grew tired of staring at the lizard. Instead he rolled over on his back and stared at the sky. Logically there would be hawks to eat the lizards. But there was no hawk, at least not right now, just a wide, pale blue sky.

Warren didn't think he was going to see much more under the sagebrush, so he came up for air. After his crawl at ground level, the sky seemed vast and the surrounding prairie endless. He let himself drift just above the sagebrush, enjoying the sense of space and the soft movement of the air.

Then he saw something odd. A grayness, a blur. It was a ghost crouching in the brush. Warren's first reaction was fear; he was seeing a ghost! Then he laughed at himself and called out, "Hi, are you from the village?"

The ghost slowly stood up. It was a skinny old man. He had a long neck threaded with tendons and bristly cheeks. His chest looked like coat hangers wrapped in tissue. He was naked.

CHAPTER TWENTY-FOUR:
Invitation to the Dance

The Naked Man had been watching Warren for quite some time. He saw Warren leave town and drift up the long slope of the prairie. He watched Warren sink into the sagebrush, and he kept on watching, waiting for Warren to emerge. When, after a considerable pause, Warren did not reappear, he grew curious. So he wended his way cautiously through the bushes, slowly, until he could just glimpse Warren's gray form wandering around just above ground level.

He wondered if Warren had lost something. But what could that be? No one had car keys or a cell phone. He moved closer.

He saw Warren stop and stare at the base of a sagebrush for a long time. Warren stared at the bush, and The Naked Man stared at Warren.

Then Warren surfaced like a dolphin breaking a wave. The Naked Man was not prepared for Warren's sudden surge skyward. He hastily crouched down into a bush.

Warren hung suspended in the air.

"Hi there!" Warren called out.

The Naked Man stood up, embarrassed.

"We wondered where you were." Warren drifted closer, still airborne. He stopped a polite distance away, within talking range, but not so close as to infringe on The Naked Man's privacy.

"Oh, yeah, I've just been out here." The Naked Man shrugged, looking at his feet.

"Are you OK?" Warren asked.

The Naked Man thought about that. No, he wasn't OK. He wasn't OK at all. But he didn't want to say so to a stranger.

"I'm alright," he said. He checked Warren's face. Warren was looking at him with pity tinged with amusement.

"I'm alright!" The Naked Man insisted. "I've been living with the cows."

"The cows! Really?" Warren lit up with interest. "How do you live with them?" He moved closer, to a friendlier distance. The Naked Man crouched down a bit, so that only his upper body showed above the bushes.

"Well, they are nice," he explained. It was true that the cows were kind. They were gentle and friendly. At night they let him cuddle up. He liked the feeling of their breath going in and out from under their rough hides. The cows felt alive in a way that he did not.

"I'm curious," Warren said, "I have been trying to figure out how this place works from an ecological point of view. That's what I was doing back there." He gestured behind him. "You were probably wondering."

"Yeah, I was, sort of."

"I was looking to see what kind of animals live here, insects and so on. I found a lizard."

"I have seen lizards. I think the animals are ghosts, too, though."

"You do? They seem corporal to some extent. More than we are."

"Well, most of the cows have crushed-in foreheads—from the slaughterhouse. That's why they're scared of people, and why they stay up here." The Naked Man waved a hand, indicating the upper prairie. "It took awhile before they would accept me."

"Really!" Warren was fascinated. He wondered what Dean had died of. Dean always looked skinny, and his fur was rough, but he had no visible wounds, except for the hole in his ear. And the cats? They were a rough-looking bunch of strays, but none looked injured. On the other hand, he had not really looked at the cats. Was Limbo populated by animals people had killed?

That didn't explain the lizard, surely. Or the insects. He needed more time to research further. But there was something else he needed to do.

"Hey, if you like living with the cows, that's great, but if you want to come back to town, your room is still there. And a couple of people are organizing a party. You might enjoy that." Warren tried to smile in an inviting way. It took effort, even though he genuinely felt sorry for The Naked Man. He just wasn't used to the role of rescuer of the marginalized.

The Naked Man hunched his shoulders shyly.

"Look," said Warren, "don't worry about that. We will get used to it. There's a lady that has her hair in curlers, and The Preacher is half naked. We are all just gray matter of some kind."

"I don't know." The Naked Man smiled sadly. "My wife always told me I shouldn't sleep in the altogether."

"Yeah, well if I had known there was an afterlife, I would have died wearing my leather jacket and my favorite jeans," Warren laughed. "Here's an idea. Why don't you show me the cows, and afterwards come back to town? If you want to?"

"OK." The Naked Man smiled shyly.

"I'm Warren. Glad to meet you."

"I'm Charles. Believe it or not, I used to be a pharmacist."

"Hey, I'll believe just about anything."

CHAPTER TWENTY-FIVE:

Awkward Visit

A lyse went to visit The Chinese Lady. On the surface, the purpose of her visit was to extend an invitation to the proposed party, but Alyse knew she wanted more than that. She imaged herself trying to communicate the concept of a party to The Chinese Lady. The Chinese Lady would have no idea what she meant. They'd end up just grinning at each other, smiling until their faces hurt, trying to communicate something else altogether. And that something else was her real agenda. She wanted to be liked by The Chinese Lady and the little boy.

She also wanted The Chinese Lady and the little boy to feel more welcome in the village. She didn't like to think of them isolated on the edge of town, maybe just to disappear one day like The Naked Man. So she made her way up the dirt street between the dusty brown buildings on a mission of friendliness.

It was one of those afternoons when a dense fog-like silence descended on the village. No one was out in the street visiting with anyone else. No one was up on a rooftop observing nature or catching a breeze. Everyone was inside somewhere, each alone with his or her own thoughts and feelings.

The only activity Alyse was aware of, other than the pecking of chickens and the skittish lurking of cats, was the lazy circling of a hawk in the sky.

In the quiet of the village, Alyse felt her confidence leaking away. She felt conspicuous, as if her activity was somehow a violation of village norms.

Nervousness made her hurry. She fled down the road to the straggled end of the village where the larger buildings degenerated into lopsided shacks. The Chinese Lady's shack was particularly humble, barely more than sticks and boards loosely attached with rusted nails, set at a little distance from the dirt road, surrounded by sagebrush.

The Chinese Lady was not out in front of her shack. She was not looking out her window. She was not visible at all. Somehow Alyse had expected The Chinese Lady to be there to greet her. She had imagined smiles and maybe hugs and cheerful attempts to communicate. Instead she found herself surrounded by a heavy wall of silence. Alyse hung in the street, wondering what to do.

Then she heard the sound of laughter. The sound was startling, like breaking glass. Alyse's heart jumped in her chest.

The little boy was laughing at something. He was on the far side of the shack, out of sight, but she could imagine the scene: The Chinese Lady and the little boy smiling together, maybe hugging each other. Alyse wanted to laugh, too. She wanted to be hugged and loved. She wanted to sob her heart out against her mother's shoulder.

Alyse began to cry. The crying caught her by surprise; she had pictured herself as part of a circle of inclusion with The Chinese Lady and the child. Instead she was falling to pieces out in the street.

Alyse began a slow backward retreat. She didn't want to interrupt the joy shared by the child and The Chinese Lady. She didn't want to make a fool of herself by crying in front of them. She was just turning to leave when the little boy flew around the side of the house, shouting with laughter, chasing a cat. At the sight of Alyse he swept to a halt, swaying in the air. He hung open-mouthed, then cried out, calling to The Chinese Lady. She emerged from the back of the shack, smiling as always.

Alyse stuttered, "Hello." She nodded and smiled, blinking the tears away, trapped and embarrassed.

The Chinese Lady returned her greeting with a slight bow. Alyse kept smiling back, feeling her cheeks stretch. They smiled and nodded at each other while the little boy watched warily. Their conversational difficulties were worse than Alyse had expected: nods and smiles and smiles and nods, while Alyse tried to get her feelings under control. Alyse realized that they would keep nodding and smiling indefinitely if she didn't think of some way to move their communication along. So she pointed at herself and said "Alyse."

More nods and smiles. The Chinese Lady pointed at her and said something like "Aiss," pointed at herself and said something like "Ay Ling," and pointed at the boy and said something like "Mahdi."

They all pointed and said each other's names over and over, nodding and smiling. Alyse felt stupid. Her face was beginning to hurt from all the smiling. She got an idea.

She picked up a little rock and drew a hopscotch on the dirt. Then she gestured to the little boy to watch. She tossed the stone, and, poised on one leg, began to hop.

But, as a ghost, mere hopping was too easy. She made her hops exaggerated, huge leaps into the air. Then she added a somersault to her hop, then did the splits. With a final pinwheel she dismounted, and, with a flourish of her arm, indicated that it was the boy's turn.

He looked a little askance, but gave it a try. A big hop up, a big hop with flapping arms, a hop up and head over heels.

Alyse and The Chinese Lady laughed and clapped. Their clapping made no sound which made them laugh more. Mahdi's face wrinkled into an elfin grin.

Then The Chinese Lady tried. She was awkward and inhibited, but got some altitude. A bit of breeze caught her and blew her off course so that she landed outside the hopscotch board. Embarrassed, she held her hand over her mouth. Mahdi flew up to her and grabbed her hand. She let her hand sink into his head, and they smiled up at each other. Alyse felt suddenly very alone.

And that's when she got her brilliant idea.

CHAPTER TWENTY-SIX:
Burning Bush

*L*ily did not like the countryside. She had decided, as a young girl, that she was not going to grow up to be a farmer's wife or live in a rural village; she was going to get out and see the world. She'd succeeded. Her travels had included Japan, Germany, and several locations in America before Scotty left the service. All of her travels had been from one urban area to another. Now she had made a trip back to a village surrounded by nothing, and she didn't like it.

She spent most of her time in the saloon, hoping that someone would come by to visit. She was good at small talk, could chatter inanely for hours, complaining mostly, but also commenting on everyone and everything. She liked to tell stories about traveling, the places she'd been, the odd aspects of local food or other customs.

If no one came by to visit, she'd set out for a wander up and down the main street. Darla was always good for a chat. Sometimes she'd run into Emmanuel. He was harder to talk to, so formal. And he didn't like gossip. Plus he had the bad habit of giving unwanted advice. Sometimes she'd run into The Preacher and say something about his sermon to get him started because once he got started he was like the radio, he just went on and on. She didn't think he actually had much to teach, but she preferred listening to him than listening to the sound of the wind blowing outside the saloon.

Sometimes there would be no one around when she went for a walk, as if everyone in town had gotten depressed at the same time.

It was on one of those depressed days, when no one came to visit, that Lily saw Scotty crying behind Trey's shack.

She set out as usual, up the middle of the dusty street, eyes roaming, looking for someone, anyone, but she saw nothing but busted out windows and shadows. The sun had bleached out the colors of Limbo to an indeterminate shade of muddy brown, with the shadows nearly black. The world was as stark as her mood.

She got clear down to the end of town without seeing a single soul, not even a chicken or a cat. Then, at the ragged edge where the village crumbled into lopsided shacks, and the lopsided shacks crumbled into piles of bramble-covered boards, she heard someone crying. The sound was coming from behind Trey's shack.

At first Lily felt annoyed. There was no point in crying about anything. Not where people could hear it. Crying in public was like begging.

But the weeping person was hidden, not seeking attention. It was private crying, the kind she preferred. So she decided to find out who it was.

She gently floated around the side of Trey's shack. She expected to find Trey in the back yard, but the hunched-over sobbing figure was not him.

It was Scotty.

He was rocking back and forth with his hands merged together in his lap, like someone in great pain.

Lily retreated out of sight.

Scotty crying. That asshole, feeling sorry for himself. She had a lot of stored up angry thoughts about Scotty. She had spent a considerable amount of time thinking those thoughts in the past, and, in truth, had not yet stopped thinking them. Lily was ready to count out her grievances like beads of a rosary right then and there in the dust and sunlight, but an unfamiliar reluctance filled her.

Asshole. Drunken bum. What's he got to whine about? she asked herself. But she had no anger left to hold onto. She just felt tired. What was the point of thinking angry thoughts about Scotty? She had other things on her mind. She didn't need to spend time being mad at that sad sack loser.

Besides, she'd been crying herself. Not that she would ever tell Scotty that.

That's when she found the charcoal. Right there in the dirt beside Trey's cabin, half covered, a burnt-up sagebrush bush reduced to a pile of charcoal.

She reached out her hand to touch the burnt wood, barely able to believe her eyes.

She needed charcoal so she could change her closet into a chapel. She had experimented with wood to no avail. Most of the sticks lying around in the brush were twisted up hunks of dead sage, suitable for clubbing Scotty, but not right for making a cross. She had tried drawing on the wall with dirt, but the wall and the dirt were about the same color. She needed charcoal, but to her knowledge there had never been a fire anywhere near the village. They had no way to start one.

And there on the edge of town, on the edge of the prairie, was a sagebrush bush that had burned long ago. Charcoal.

She stared at the blacked chunks of burned wood with her hands pressed into her chest. It was a miracle. She was certain of that. The first miracle of her life. She had prayed before. She had asked for children, had asked that Scotty stop drinking and stop beating on her, had asked that Scotty die so she would be free of him. God had never given her anything before, but now, suddenly, He had given her charcoal.

Lily couldn't wait to reach her closet. She gathered as much charcoal as she could hold, which wasn't much, just two or three tiny pieces in each hand. Then she flew down the street, took a tight corner at speed to enter the saloon, and came to an abrupt stop.

She had to do this right. She had to have the right frame of mind.

Lily hung in the air of the saloon. She made herself breathe slowly. She tried to feel humble. She felt gratitude. She let the gratitude in, let it swell her heart. Holding the gratitude in her chest like an offering, she crept slowly toward her closet.

Lily left the closet door open to allow the light in. She knelt and hardened her legs so she could feel the rough wood splintery against her shins. She tried to put aside her fear of failure; art was not her thing. She didn't draw, not even stick figures. She tried to picture a cross as something more than just two lines at right angles. She would not attempt to draw a crucified Jesus.

She took in a shaky breath and touched the charcoal lightly onto the wall. It made a mark. She stopped, frightened. Her cross would not be good enough. She needed to ask around to see if anyone was artistic and willing to make one for her. No. She didn't want to tell anyone about her chapel. They would just make fun of her: Warren and Jack and them. How anyone could be a non-believer in Limbo, she could not imagine. But they were, and she didn't want them to know about her chapel.

She drew a shaky line. Then she made a right angle turn and drew another line. Slowly she outlined a cross.

It looked terrible. The lines were wriggly and uncertain. The cross piece was longer on one side than the other. It tilted like an old gravestone. Lily felt tears pushing against her eyes.

"I'm sorry. I will fix it."

She tired again. She retraced the lines, adding a little on each side to make the lines longer and straighter. She added a little to the short cross piece. It looked better, more balanced. But barren, just straight lines.

Lily widened the lines, making them curve slightly,

making the cross softer, the corners rounded. She sat back. The cross looked complete. It looked gentle, as if drawn in smoke.

Lily began to cry. She rocked back and forth with her hands pressed into her face.

"Thank you thank you thank you."

CHAPTER TWENTY-SEVEN:
Let's Party

Alyse cleared her throat and rubbed her hands together. "OK, let's . . . " No one was listening to her except Trey and maybe Scotty.

"Hey, people!" she yelled. Heads turned. She saw Warren watching her with a faint smile. The Preacher broke off a conversation with Emmanuel.

Alyse tossed her hair back over her shoulder and stood as tall as she could. She was on the boardwalk in front of the saloon, which gave her a little height. The other villagers were milling around in the street. They were behaving like atoms, some attracting others to form sociable molecules, some repelling others. Alyse realized that the party could fizzle out if she didn't change the mood.

"Come on up," she called, "come up closer." She made gathering motions with her arms. The strays on the edge moved in. One was Lily, who seemed oddly vulnerable outside of the saloon, like a snail with no shell. Darla was an outlier as well, but on the opposite side of the crowd. She was pissed, Alyse thought, because she was not running the show.

The crowd did not look like people who were about to have a party. Some of them looked like they were about to get into a fight, some looked curious, some bored, some looked ready to leave. Alyse's friends were loyally gathered front and center: Trey, Scotty, Warren, Traveling Jack, and Ay Ling and Mahdi.

She forced enthusiasm into her voice. "Welcome to the first Limbo neighborhood block party! Trey and I are so glad you all came!"

She paused for a response. There were some murmurs and a subdued cheer from Jack that might have been sarcastic.

"This is our first party," Alyse sang out with forced cheerfulness, "and we hope to have more! But for this first party we have three things planned. The first is an ice breaker so we can get to know each other better."

She could tell that was not going over well. The ghosts glanced sideways at each other and the murmuring grew.

"It's just a game," Alyse explained, trying not to sound defensive. "It goes like this: I am going to tell you something about myself that none of you know. Then I will point at one of you and then you tell us something that no one knows about you. And so on. And when we are done, we will all know each other a little better."

Jack groaned.

"You have to form a circle to do this." Alyse forged

on bravely. She made herding motions with her arms. The ghosts reluctantly shifted and shuffled into a circle. Alyse could feel the party dying.

Warren stepped up. "I'd like to start," he said. "Is that OK?"

Alyse smiled gratefully. Warren said, "Something that none of you know about me is that I have a daughter."

Everyone stared at him. No one quite said "So what?" but they could feel the words hanging in the air. They were all exiled from loved ones.

"She would be a teenager by now," Warren explained. His voice was carefully controlled. "I don't know her. She was born when her mother and I were in high school, and she was given up for adoption. But the point is, I hope she grows up to be a girl like Alyse."

Alyse's mouth opened in surprise. Warren swept a bow and doffed an imaginary hat. "So let's thank Alyse for this party!" People mumbled "thank you's" and shifted around in embarrassment.

Warren saved Alyse the difficulty of a response by pointing to Darla. "I'd like to know something about you, Darla."

He caught her off guard. Darla quickly wiped the look of resentment from her face and pasted on her public smile. She hesitated, thinking, and for one moment she looked vulnerable and genuine. Then she stepped forward and announced, "Well, here's an unknown fact about me. None of you know that I was a state champion baton twirler in the great state of Iowa when I was in high school!" She threw an imaginary baton up in the air and caught it with a flourish.

"Yeah, Darla!" Alyse hollered. Suddenly she could see Darla as a high school student, rather than as a PTA lady. Trey cheered, too, and Emmanuel called out "Good for you!" They were trying to pump up the party, get the right spirit moving.

Darla pointed at Emmanuel. "Why don't you go next? I'm sure you can share something special."

Emmanuel thought for a minute and then launched into a story about his friendship with the neighborhood cows of his childhood. It had been his job as a child to keep them away from the front of his father's store. He could have driven them away with shouts or blows with a stick, but instead he sang to them. The cows followed him when he sang. He led them away from the front door like the Pied Piper. "I am not known as an animal lover," he concluded, "but I do like cows."

There was a spatter of low grade cheering for Emmanuel. Most of the ghosts could not picture him as child in Ghana, singing to cows. It was hard to imagine him as a child at all. Still, they loved his singing and appreciated his story.

He chose Lily to speak next. She said she didn't like animals and didn't understand why they had to be here in Limbo with the humans, or why they had a happier afterlife. No one was surprised by her statement, but they applauded her for telling them, anyway. She pointed at Traveling Jack and said, "Your turn. Tell us all about you."

Jack sauntered out to the middle of the street and gazed up at the sky. "Weellll," he drawled, "I bet you all think you know all about me already." There were a few snickers from the crowd. "You all think I'm just some old hippie who was too stoned all the time to even be able to remember being alive, right?" He let his gaze roam through the crowd. "Yep, I did smoke some awesome weed in my time. But there is something none of you know." He paused for dramatic affect. "I have something important in common with Keith Richards of the Rolling Stones!"

Scotty moaned and Trey yelled, "That ain't no surprise!"

"You haven't heard yet what it is." Jack made sure he had their attention before he dropped his punch line. "What Keith Richards and I have in common is we were both Boy Scouts."

Someone shouted with laughter and Lily yelled, "What did you smoke around the campfire?"

"I was a genuine uniform-wearing old-lady-helping Boy Scout when I was a kid, just like Keith Richards." Jack bowed elaborately to the audience. "And now you know something about me that you didn't know before."

Jack's performance received a rousing ovation.

Jack strolled back to the circle of ghosts. On his way he gave a nod to The Preacher. Lily saw the nod and hollered, "Preach it, Preacher!" Someone groaned.

The Preacher hesitated, then drifted slowly toward the center of the circle. He knew he could not outperform Jack, not at a party, not in front of Jack's friends. Or perhaps it was Lily's jeering and the groan that kept The Preacher from launching into a long-winded story about his religious experiences. Instead, after a pause for thought, he told them a story about being the fastest runner in his high school. No one believed his claim, but they applauded anyway. The atmosphere of the party had changed; the ghosts were in a mood to cheer anyone for anything.

The Preacher picked Trey to speak next. Trey said that he used to be really good at making homemade BBQ sauce, and everyone cheered because everyone liked Trey. He pointed at The Chinese Lady.

Alyse, speaking for Ay Ling, told them about her garden. Ay Ling smiled and bowed even though she didn't know what Alyse had said. Loud cheering followed; a rollicking mood had taken over.

They continued around the circle, cheering revelations from each ghost, until they were all the way around with only Scotty left. With everyone staring at him, Scotty shrank into himself. Alyse smiled encouragingly at him. "Your turn, Scotty!"

He shifted uncomfortably, then said, "I guess my life didn't amount to much, but, well, now that I've stopped drinking, I know something I didn't know before." He paused, squared his shoulders and said, "I still love you, Lily. I always will."

Lily glared, unimpressed. "That and a buck wouldn't buy me a cup of coffee."

The villagers mumbled their discomfort. It didn't seem like cheering was an appropriate response. To cover, Warren called out, "Hey, we're missing someone."

He looked up at the window of the saloon. "Charles," he yelled, "come down here."

Who? Everyone looked around, then followed Warren's eyes up to the window. The Naked Man appeared, hunched over, grinning shyly. "Come on down!" Warren called. "Come and meet everyone."

It took a minute or two. Then The Naked Man emerged through the wall of the saloon, sideways, with one hand over his crotch. They all looked, while trying not to be seen looking. There really wasn't much to see, side on.

"Hi, everyone," said The Naked Man.

He edged into the circle next to Warren. Scotty tried to slap his back, but his hand swung all the way through. "Good to meetcha!"

There was a general outbreak of "hello's" and "hi there's" from the villagers. Charles ducked his head in embarrassment.

"Well, thank you for joining us," Alyse said. "Please tell us something about you."

"I guess you already know that I slept in my birthday suit," Charles joked, and everyone laughed just a little too loudly.

"Well, I could tell you just about anything and you'd believe it since none of you know much about me. Uh . . . before I died I didn't have pets or anything, but now I know the cows really well. I'm like that gentleman over there . . . I like cows. They are very nice animals. I have been living with them out there in the . . . " He waved a hand toward the prairie. "Out there." He shrugged bashfully. Everyone cheered, not because he was a friend of cows, but to make him feel welcome.

"There!" Alyse applauded, "Wasn't that nice? Now we all know each other a little better!" The crowd had changed; from random atoms they had become a molecule, everyone smiling.

Alyse smiled back at them and then, with a flourish, introduced Trey.

"So . . . here's our other host for today, Trey! Trey, you're up."

Trey moved into the center of the circle as Alyse retreated, bowing. Trey looked around slowly, his head bobbling like a dashboard toy. "Hi y'all, glad you all came to this party. Now I'm gonna need for you to gather over here on the sidewalk, right over this way, so you can look up at the sky over there." He pointed up in the air.

Everyone reshuffled themselves into a row in front of the wooden boardwalk.

Alyse took Mahdi's hand, and they flew out to the middle of the road. There they hovered side by side.

"I present to you. . . " Trey tried to ham it up a bit, ". . . Alyse and Mahdi, the amazing Limbo Air Dancers!"

Alyse caught Mahdi's eye and nodded her encouragement. The little boy's face wrinkled into a grin. Alyse began a whispered chant. "One hundred and one, one hundred and one, one hundred and one . . . "

They rose up in the air together, touching only with fingertips, arms out, legs straight, toes pointed. Then slowly they pinwheeled apart in opposite directions. The pinwheels turned into somersaults, then into slow spins. With no music but wind, birdsong and Alyse's chanting, their dance was odd, but interesting. They kept an eye on each other and danced as mirror images. They did a set of parallel spins like figure skaters. They did head stands. They did back flips and forward flips. Then they did a final pinwheel toward each other, ending with touching finger tips.

Alyse's eyes met Mahdi's and they chanted together softly, "One hundred and one, one hundred and one, one hundred and one." On the last word, they shot upwards, holding hands, until they were only visible as black dots against the blue sky.

From the sky high above the village, Alyse could see all of the ghosts arranged in a loose circle in the street. They looked like dust, their faces indistinguishable. Alyse had a sudden urge to cry, but a different kind of crying; she felt a swelling in her heart. She turned to Mahdi and grabbed him in an unscripted hug.

Mahdi buried his face in her chest and they floated together, merged. Then, remembering that they were supposed to be dancing, Alyse released him. "Ready?" Alyse asked. Her smile was tremulous. Mahdi didn't understand English words, but knew what she meant. Alyse tossed her hair back, sucked in a deep breath of satisfaction and said, "Let's go!" They swan-dived together down to the ground and landed in tandem. Then they bowed to their audience.

The villagers yelled their approval and clapped their hands in that strange silent applause that was one of the hallmarks of Limbo. Mahdi ran to The Chinese Lady for a hug. Alyse flew to Trey, smiling ear to ear, and he gave her an awkward side hug. "That was real pretty," Trey said. Alyse could not stop bouncing with jubilation.

Trey, grinning at her antics, moved out to the middle of the street and called for the attention of the villagers.

"OK, people. That was a great dance from Alyse and Mahdi. And now we will have a song from Emmanuel. Come on up, Emmanuel."

"Thank you." Emmanuel moved forward as Trey and Alyse joined the watching villagers. Somehow, even barefoot and in his pj's, Emmanuel gave the appearance of wearing a suit. He breathed in and out, settling himself. He had performed before, mostly in churches, to audiences dressed for the occasion. Now, hovering over the dusty street, he studied his audience. The villagers looked like a collection of faded rags with faces, but they were faces he knew, and he felt a kind of affection for them. They were settling down, focusing on him, waiting for him. He could not disappoint.

He pulled a deep note from the heart of his chest.

"My life flows on in endless song . . . "

He had a big voice, one that could fill a room. In the street, with the light breeze, his voice became a wind that blew through his listeners. He played out each word and each note deliberately.

"Above earth's lamentations..."

He sang three verses. He felt his voice moving through his chest and through the listening people. He could see the effect on their faces. They were following intently, some making small lifting motions when his voice rose, some moving their mouths as if they wanted to sing along.

Then he spoke to them. "We are going to sing the first verse again, together. Since you don't know the words, we will sing it line by line. I hope you will sing along. Since I cannot remember the words I was taught, I am using some of my own."

"My life flows on in endless song
 Above earth's laminations . . . "

He stopped singing and listened. The voices of the villagers were tentative and shy, like the sound of leaves in the wind, as they repeated the line of song.

Emmanuel sang:

"I hear a real, though far off, tune
That hails a new creation."

The villagers repeated the line with more confidence.

"Above the tumult and the strife
I hear its music winging . . . "

Emmanuel let his voice ring out like a bell, giving them the last line. Then he raised his arms like an orchestra conductor and the whole village sang together.

"Since God has love for all of life
How can I keep from singing?"

CHAPTER TWENTY-EIGHT:
Morning and Evening After

Trey and Alice sat on her front steps in companionable silence. Alyse was watching swallows play, and Trey was thinking of his grandkids.

Alice wondered if she and Mahdi could make a show based on swallows. She imagined herself and Mahdi performing for a happy crowd—the Limbo Air Dancers' second performance! It would be hard to top the first.

The party had been pathetic in a way, that ragged crowd of ghosts, trying to clap. But everyone had enjoyed it. They really had.

"Hey, Trey," she said. "The party was a success, wasn't it?"

"Yeah, it was."

She smiled, and he smiled back.

"Hey, look," Alyse laughed.

A straggly parade of chickens approached them, wandering out of the sagebrush. They gathered in Alyse's front yard. Alyse was delighted, Trey less so.

"I'll keep them as pets," she said.

Trey studied the chickens skeptically. "They seem pretty good at looking after themselves."

"They can sleep in the house and be safe from coyotes." Alyse only needed a brief acquaintance with the chickens to become attached to them.

"Here, chickie, chickie, chickie," she called. She held out her hand to a large bronze and black hen. The hen, interrupted from her foraging, stood up to her full height and fixed Alyse with a beady-eyed glare.

Alyse withdrew her hand.

"I guess that one don't want to be friends," said Trey.

"Well, maybe later," Alyse said, unperturbed. The chickens had definitely chosen to move into her territory with her. A few continued to forage, but most of them nestled down in the dust, as comfortable as tea cozies.

"They have made themselves at home," Trey commented.

Alyse propped her chin in her hands. They sat in a friendly silence, watching the hens.

Then Alyse said, "I don't feel so bad about being here any more."

"Because of the party?"

"Partly. I mean that was nice, especially Emmanuel's singing. And I really like Mahdi and Ay Ling. But I just mean in general."

"Do you remember what Warren said? About hoping his daughter would be like you?"

"Yeah," Alyse grimaced, "I was kind of embarrassed."

Trey stared off into the distance, "I kinda feel that way. I feel like you are the daughter I wished I'd had."

Alyse felt gratitude bloom in her chest, like a flower. "Trey, I'd be honored to be your daughter." Their hands merged. They smiled shyly at each other.

Later that night Alyse did not talk to her parents and sister. She didn't imagine that she could look into their home and watch them go about their activities. Instead, she curled up around a glowing warmth in her chest and told herself: My mom and dad and Andee still love me. I miss them, but I still love them, and I am still loved by them. We will always love each other.

I was lucky, she thought. I had a good life.

She hoped that Mahdi was tucked into Ay Ling's arms to sleep. She hoped The Preacher wasn't lonely, and that Lily would find what she was looking for. She wished that Darla and Scotty could be a little happier. She wished that everyone could feel loved.

She pressed her hands together as if praying and whispered, "Good night, everyone. Sweet dreams."

CHAPTER TWENTY-NINE:
Five Card Draw

"Ante up." Pebbles rattled on the wooden floor. It was Jack's deal. He glanced around the circle. "Looks like we have two new players in Lily's House of Cards. Welcome to the game, suckers."

Lily made a snorting noise. Scotty hunched apologetically. He was a rounded gray presence at the game, like a large dust bunny, sitting opposite Lily. Charles sat beside him, also hunched over and embarrassed.

"Get ready to get skinned." Jack skimmed out the cards face down.

"Looks like he got skinned already," Lily sneered across the circle at Charles. "Ha!"

"Charles can't help that." Warren laid his hand on his cards, holding them down to the table. "Shouldn't we wait for Trey and Alyse?"

"My friends call me Charlie," said The Naked Man. He lifted his chin with a touch of defiance.

Warren nodded in acknowledgement. "Charlie. Anyone seen Trey or Alyse this morning?"

"Trey was gone when I woke up," Scotty told them. "He must have gone over to Alyse's early."

Jack shrugged impatiently. "We can deal them in when they get here. Alrighty, then, read 'em and weep!"

CHAPTER THIRTY:
A Dog's Afterlife

Dean trotted past the saloon. He knew Warren was in there doing whatever it was humans did with their time, some incomprehensible activity that did not interest him. He was interested in the smell of chickens.

He followed the chicken scent down the road to the edge of town. And there they were, pecking in the grass outside an unoccupied shack. He stopped to watch awhile. He liked the clucking of the chickens, the way they constantly chattered with each other, a conversation that seemed to be endless affirmations of their unity.

It would be nice to have another dog for company. But he had the ghosts, so he wasn't too lonely.

And his world was full of enticing scents: cows, pigs, and yes, there it was . . . a rabbit! Dean let out a yodeling howl of glee. He set out at a purposeful lope into the landscape.

Once out in the sagebrush, Dean broke into an all-out run, zigging and zagging around and through the shrubbery. He enjoyed the long loose feel of his muscles in action. He could feel the heat of the sun on his back and the sweet cooling wind on his face. He loved the smell of sagebrush, sharp and intoxicating, though not as alluring as the scent of rabbit. His tongue lolled out. His breath rolled in and out in satisfying surges, filling him with a sense of freedom.

He felt boundlessly alive and could not keep from singing out in long, loud, dog yowls as he ran.

THE End

AUTHOR
Acknowledgments

Abig Thank You to my editors and proofreaders, Tamira Thayne and Cayr Ariel Wulff, for helping my tale become as error-free and fluid as they possibly could. And, to my sister, Anne, who reads everything I write. You have my gratitude.

ABOUT THE
Author

*L*aura Koerber is an artist and writer who lives on an island with her husband and two dogs. Laura divides her retirement time between dog rescue, care for disabled people, political activism, and yes, she tells herself stories while driving. Her first book, *The Dog Thief and Other Stories* (written as Jill Kearney), was listed by Kirkus Review as one of the Hundred Best Books of 2015. She's also the author of *The Listener's Tale, I Once Was Lost, But Now I'm Found, Limbo,* and the upcoming *Shapeshifter's Tale.*

Thank you for taking the time to read Limbo.

COULD YOU TAKE A MOMENT TO GIVE THE BOOK
A SHORT REVIEW ON AMAZON.COM? YOUR REVIEWS
MEAN THE WORLD TO OUR AUTHORS, AND HELP
STORIES SUCH AS THIS ONE REACH A WIDER
AUDIENCE. THANK YOU SO MUCH!

Find links to
Limbo
AND ALL OUR GREAT BOOKS
ON AMAZON OR AT WWW.WHOCHAINSYOU.COM.

Also from Laura Koerber

I ONCE WAS LOST, BUT NOW I'M FOUND: DAISY AND THE OLYMPIC ANIMAL SANCTUARY RESCUE

On the far side of the Olympic Peninsula in Washington State, halfway between the mountains and the ocean, stands the little town of Forks. In that town, in a quiet neighborhood of modest homes and shabby businesses, there remains a dilapidated pink warehouse.

Packed inside that warehouse, living in deplorable conditions, were once over 120 dogs. In one of the crates was a black dog named Daisy. This is her story.

It is also the story of the rescue of one hundred and twenty-four dogs—and one snake—from the Olympic Animal Sanctuary, the only large-scale dog rescue in the U.S. to be carried out with no support from local government. The OAS rescue was an epic narrative that extended over several years and featured small town politics, protests, assault, lawsuits, arrests, and a midnight escape, all played out to a nationwide audience.

...Read more and order from whochainsyou.com, Amazon, and other outlets.

Also from Laura Koerber

THE DOG THIEF AND OTHER STORIES
WRITING AS JILL KEARNEY

"**D**ecrepit humans rescue desperate canines, cats and the occasional rat in this collection of shaggy but piercing short stories."

Listed by Kirkus Review as one of the best books of 2015, this collection of short stories and a novella explores the complexity of relationships between people and animals in an impoverished rural community where the connections people have with animals are sometimes their only connection to life.

According to Kirkus Review: "Kearney treats her characters, and their relationships with their pets, with a cleareyed, unsentimental sensitivity and psychological depth. Through their struggles, she shows readers a search for meaning through the humblest acts of caretaking and companionship. A superb collection of stories about the most elemental of bonds."...*Read more and order from whochainsyou.com, Amazon, and other outlets.*

Also from Laura Koerber

THE LISTENER'S TALE

Anna didn't even know she had an aunt. Aunt Moira had appeared the day after Anna's parents died in a car crash: a tall grey figure through the screen door, silhouetted against the bright sun. The neighbors welcomed her—they were relieved to get Anna off their hands and into the custody of a relative.

But Anna hadn't warmed to her aunt or her pug, whose eyes eerily tracked Anna's every move. Something wasn't right; her investigation leads to a world she's never seen and even more relatives who live in a quirky village—a village where singers dance in the sky, the elders are hundreds of years old, and everyone has access to magic.

At first bemused, then charmed, Anna settles in to live with her new-found relations—and unravel the mystery of who is trying to kill her.

The Listener's Tale is a fantasy for young teen readers or the young at heart....*Read more and order from whochainsyou.com, Amazon, and other outlets.*

About Who Chains You Books

WELCOME TO WHO CHAINS YOU: BOOKS FOR THOSE WHO BELIEVE PEOPLE—AND ANIMALS— DESERVE TO BE FREE.

At Who Chains You Books our mission is a simple one—to amplify the voices of the animals through the empowerment of animal lovers, activists, and rescuers to write and publish books elevating the status of animals in today's society.

We hope you'll visit our website and join us on this adventure we call animal advocacy publishing. We welcome you.

Read more about us at whochainsyou.com.

Made in the USA
Lexington, KY
14 December 2017